# NEW WINE

## *Transportation*

# COMPANY

*A SPRINGVILLE STORY*

# NEW WINE

## Transportation

# COMPANY

*A Springville Story*

AUTHOR OF *WHERE I WAS PLANTED*

# HEATHER NORMAN SMITH

## AMBASSADOR INTERNATIONAL
GREENVILLE, SOUTH CAROLINA & BELFAST, NORTHERN IRELAND

www.ambassador-international.com

# New Wine Transportation Company
## A Springville Story

ISBN: 978-1-64960-056-1
eISBN: 978-1-64960-057-8
Library of Congress Control Number: 2021932453

Cover design by Hannah Linder Designs
Interior Typesetting by Dentelle Design
Digital Edition by Anna Riebe Raats
Edited by Katie Cruice Smith

This is a work of fiction. Names, characters, and incidents are all products of the author's imagination or are used for fictional purposes. Any resemblance to actual events or persons, living or dead, is entirely coincidental. Any mentioned brand names, places, and trademarks remain the property of their respective owners, bear no association with the author or the publisher, and are used for fictional purposes only.

Scripture taken from the King James Version (Public Domain) and from the New King James Version®. Copyright © 1982 by Thomas Nelson. Used by permission. All rights reserved.

AMBASSADOR INTERNATIONAL
Emerald House
411 University Ridge, Suite B14
Greenville, SC 29601, USA
www.ambassador-international.com

AMBASSADOR BOOKS
The Mount
2 Woodstock Link
Belfast, BT6 8DD, Northern Ireland, UK
www.ambassadormedia.co.uk

*The colophon is a trademark of Ambassador, a Christian publishing company.*

## Dedication

To all the "characters" in the region I call home—the people of
the North Carolina communities, towns, villages, and cities that
have, with all their charms and wonders, marked my heart with
the notion that there is no better place to be this side of Heaven.
To the residents of the northwestern Piedmont zip codes who have
amalgamated in my imagination to form the fictional town of
Springville, North Carolina.

# *Acknowledgments*

THANK YOU TO EACH OF my fellow authors who have helped promote my books and encouraged me in the writing journey and, specifically, to my fellow Ambassador International authors who brainstormed with me on Facebook when I first tossed out this crazy idea of a preacher and his ministry involving a bar. Thank you to my editor, Katie Cruice Smith, and the rest of the Ambassador International publishing team for helping me bring another Springville story to life.

Thank you to the readers of my first novel, *Grace & Lavender*, who asked to read more about the town of Springville and Springville Community Christian Church.

Thank you to my dad, Rev. Bobby Norman, who has been a minister since before I was born, for his invaluable example. He has modeled dedication to the Lord by always answering to God first and to man second, and demonstrated enduring service to a congregation, even through difficult circumstances.

I would also like to acknowledge the example set by my husband, Rev. Alex Smith, whose steadfast faith under pressure and love for his family also contributed greatly to shaping the main character in this story.

*Preface*

THIS STORY IS NOT ABOUT drinking or not drinking alcohol. It is not meant to spark a theological debate and is not intended to be a representation of my personal interpretation of Scripture on the subject of alcohol. This story is about "the love of God [that] has been poured out in our hearts by the Holy Spirit" (Rom. 5:5). It is, like all my writing, about how God works "all things together for good" (Rom. 8:28). And it is about obedience to His leading, even when our direction is challenged.

*Trust in the LORD with all your heart;*
*And lean not on your own understanding.*

*Proverbs 3:5*

*Chapter One*

ANOTHER GRAND OPENING—THIS ONE NOT so grand. At least not to some folks in Springville.

Pastor Daniel Whitefield sighed and folded the Monday edition of the tri-weekly *Springville Chronicle*, then placed it on the table with the corner tucked under the edge of his half-eaten plate of biscuits and gravy. Mumblings of the big news filtered through the greasy air of the diner. Chatter of various volumes, accompanied by clanging and clapping of silverware against plates and cups meeting tables, crossed the long room in all directions, bounced off the walls, and came to rest in his ears all at once with a heaviness. *A tizzy.* That's what his mother used to call it. People were all worked up and in a tizzy of one kind or another.

He read the headline again. "Main Street Bar Open For Business." Front page, above the fold—not the real estate most papers would give such a story. But it was big news in Springville. Beneath the article was a picture of the entire grinning chamber of commerce—five men and three women posing with a pair of giant cardboard scissors for the ceremonial ribbon cutting. And the new bar's owner—a tall, lanky man in a suit, named in the caption as a Mr. Adam Curtis—stood behind them, his hands poised in a clap, with his face just in the shadows.

Daniel brought the fork to his mouth again, loaded with a large piece of fluffy biscuit bathed in perfectly seasoned sausage gravy. Before he could swallow, a stubby pointer finger to his right and awkwardly close to his cup of coffee pressed into the tabletop and bent itself back at the first joint. The digit was colored brown with a mixture of dirt, melanin, and aged cigarette tar, and its dry skin was lined with side-to-side cracks like a carrot. Daniel swallowed the lump of biscuit down as his eyes followed the finger up toward the familiar face of its owner.

"Well, hello, Clifford. I hope you're doing well today," Daniel said. He slid the cup away from Clifford's hand, then picked it up to take a sip.

"You seen the news in the paper?" the man said gruffly.

Daniel set the coffee cup down as he drummed his fingers on the copy of the paper in front of him. His head tilted up at Clifford. "You mean about the new place opening up?"

The burly man nodded, and his lip curled on one side in a snarl. Daniel squared his shoulders.

"Yes. I had heard it was coming but I wasn't sure when. I read the article just now."

"Well, whaddaya gonna do about it, Pastor?"

His instinct was to tell six-foot-three Clifford that "pastor" was reserved for those who attended more than just three services per year, but that was certainly no way to win people over. He was still a pastor, whether he was officially Clifford's or not.

"I'm no happier about it than you seem to be, Cliff," Daniel said, "but I don't know how much we can do now except pray. It seems to be a done deal. Like the headline says, Main Street Bar is open for business."

"Well, I don't think you oughta just sit back and stay quiet. Idn't your brother-in-law some big wig for the town? Maybe you oughta talk to him 'bout what can be done."

"Richard is president of the chamber of commerce, but I don't think he—"

"And I'm sure you're on that . . . what do they call it? That *coalition* of ministers that's speakin' out agin it. *Ain't ya?*"

"Well, no. I actually hadn't heard about that until I read the article."

Clifford, who wore an orange safety vest over blue and black flannel, shrugged his shoulders. "Oh, maybe that's 'cause you jus' started workin' for 'em over at your church," he said.

"Clifford, I've pastored Springville Community Christian Church for twenty-three years! You know that."

"Yeah, but now they pay you for it." He pointed his used toothpick at the pastor as he spoke. "And I guess that means you gotta work a little harder now."

Daniel pinched his eyes closed tightly for two seconds and prayed for sanctification. He couldn't punch the man. He'd end up on the front page of the *Springville Chronicle*, too. "Local Pastor Decks Diner Patron." Worse yet, someone would surely video the aftermath with their smartphone, and he'd be an unwilling YouTube star before dinnertime. How would that be for a witness?

"Not that it is really any of your business . . . " Daniel began loudly. A pair of white-haired ladies at the next table—identical twin sisters who, until recently had both taught second grade at Springville Elementary—turned their heads at the pastor's raised voice. They stared until he quieted, and his posture relaxed when, finally, spirit overtook flesh.

"Cliff, I've always been paid by the church. The fact that *after all this time,* I was able to quit my *other* full-time job just means I have more time now to devote to my congregation. I'm not an accountant anymore—just a pastor."

"Well, I meant no harm, Preacher." The words were slow and drawn-out. Fake remorse was plastered on his face. "Just wanted to get your thoughts on the new business." He nodded and started backing away from the table.

"But you didn't even ask me my thoughts on . . . "

Clifford turned and headed for the door. A man with a Department of Transportation vest—obviously his coworker—stood there tapping his watch.

Daniel huffed and picked up the paper again. Only a brief mention of concern from the community and only a short statement about the coalition of pastors from Springville churches. He scanned the article a third time. *Adam Curtis.* The name was so familiar, but the paper said he was from two hours south, in Charlotte, and that he owned three other bars in the Queen City. Daniel certainly didn't know anyone like that.

The diner continued to buzz. This made eight. Eight grand openings downtown in as many months. Main Street had been resurrected, it seemed. After years of steady decline and more storefronts boarded up than not, downtown was suddenly alive again.

The boom started with a boutique for homemade soaps back in the summer. Not many had expected it to survive long; but against the odds, the store thrived, prompting other businesses to move to downtown Springville. Next came a shoe store and a hardware store, then a series of other retailers and services too small for right-off-the-highway space but desperately needed. But the bar was different. A place like that should have been on the outskirts of town, on the fringe, out of sight. Certainly not in the heart of Springville, North Carolina.

The white-haired ladies hadn't stopped talking about it since they sat down.

"I can't believe they're doing this, Ethel."

"You just wait and see, Mary. Springville will go down the toilet in no time."

"What happened to the wholesome place where we raised our families?"

"It makes me plumb heart-sick."

Daniel tried to block out the noise. He took the last bite of his breakfast and fought the urge to lick the plate. He put his fork down regretfully as the diner's owner eased slowly into the booth across from him—no invitation needed.

"Was he givin' you a hard time, Preacher Whitefield?"

"Clifford's always givin' people a hard time, isn't he, Speedy?" Daniel chuckled.

There was much dispute in town about the origin of the nickname. Speedy, whose given name was Theodore, was unsure himself who had started it and whether it had more to do with his quickness slinging hash or his Saturday drag racing hobby. His racing days were long over, but he could still serve up a meal like nobody's business.

Speedy gave him a knowing smile as he wiped his hands on the white apron tied around his waist. Of course, Speedy understood the way of things in Springville as good as anyone else. He'd been around a long time.

The old man pressed his forearms into the table and leaned forward just enough that Daniel felt invited to talk but not pressured.

"I'm not tryin' to judge the fella," Daniel said, "and I don't mean to talk out of turn, but I'll never understand why someone who doesn't even go to church regularly always wants to stick his nose in church business. What does it matter to him what I think about the bar? Or anything else, for that matter."

"Oh, *that* business." Speedy shook his head. "That's all I've heard about this morning. Main Street Bar this and Main Street Bar that. Some folks anxious to check it out. Some spittin' mad about it." Speedy's hands went into the air and back down. "What did Clifford say to you?"

Daniel looked down and noticed a spot of gravy on his tie. He wiped at it with a napkin as he answered.

"He seemed to think I should *do* something about it, though I can't imagine what. Unless it's to join the coalition against it." He gave up on the tie. "Speedy, I'm not happy about a bar opening up downtown, of course. No doubt we'd be better off with a bakery or a tackle shop. And I worry about what it will do for people. But I just don't understand a coalition against it."

"Seems like a lotta noise to me. It's not like we don't already have those kinds of places out near the county line."

"Yeah, I agree. I know the other preachers have the best of intentions. They're good men. And everybody wants to keep our little town respectable, but . . . people act like God's not big enough to look out for Springville. Like He's not still in control. Like the sky is falling." Daniel's voice softened. "Then again, maybe they're doing what God told them to do. Maybe He *wants* them to speak out, and maybe that's what I should do, too." He puffed air out through his nose, and his lips turned inward. "But I just haven't gotten that message yet."

"Hmm . . . " Speedy leaned back and rubbed the sparse, white whiskers on his chin. His small, dark eyes were thoughtful. "Let me ask you this, Preacher: What did you do when the barber shop opened up beside the soap store last month?"

Daniel smiled thinking about his new friends the Kostases.

"I stopped by to introduce myself; and I wished the owners well; and I invited them to come to church. And I got a haircut, even though I didn't need one."

"Well, then," Speedy said, "maybe that's what you oughta do now. Not necessarily the patronage part, but the introducin' and invitin' part."

Daniel let Speedy's words sink in as he reached into the back pocket of his slacks in slow motion for his wallet.

"You know, Speedy . . . you just might be right," Daniel said. He fished a ten out of the wallet. "I'm not sure why I didn't think of that. But I'm glad *you* did. Maybe it is just that simple. I can't go wrong by simply introducing myself and inviting someone to church. No matter who they are."

He shook the old man's hand to say goodbye and offered him a grateful smile. Speedy simultaneously winked, clicked his tongue, and formed his weathered, wrinkled fingers in a gunpoint of affirmation.

Daniel headed to the cash register, blocking out the murmurings as he went. He paid for breakfast, then stepped out into the cool, March morning air. The smile on his face stuck all the way to the car and half the way home as he thought about the diner proprietor's words.

*Sometimes, God speaks from a pulpit,* Daniel thought. *Sometimes, God speaks in the silence. And sometimes, God speaks through little, old men with dishpan hands.*

# Chapter Two

DANIEL'S PETITE, DARK-HAIRED WIFE PAUSED to rub his shoulders as she passed by the kitchen table, where he sat studying for the Wednesday night lesson. Her small fingers kneaded the tense muscles. After thirty years, she knew just how to press into the knots that formed under his shoulder blades when he was stressed; and even if it was only for a few moments, she did it almost every day, without being asked.

"This Main Street Bar business—it's tricky, isn't it?" Daniel said. He dropped his pen onto the notepad in front of him, closed his eyes, and tried to relax. The entire time he'd been studying, his mind wandered to Clifford and what he'd said at the diner. "Not everyone can understand the complexities, the real problem." He reached up and patted her hand. "Thanks. I needed that."

"It is tricky, dear." Marsha ended the impromptu massage and walked to the refrigerator. She retrieved a diet soda—her one, true vice—and closed the fridge. "But I know you'll handle it. You always do."

Such confidence she had in him. *I am a blessed man to have her in my corner,* he thought, *always cheering me on.*

The knots in his shoulders having been chased away, they reformed at the base of his neck as he stared at the open Bible. The translucent paper and tiny black type were as familiar to his eyes as his own hand; but as he read the first chapter of the book of James, the fifth verse seemed to lift off the page and beg for his attention.

*If any of you lacks wisdom, let him ask of God, who gives to all liberally and without reproach, and it will be given to him.*[1]

*Let him ask.* He'd prayed half the way home from the diner. Then again before he began studying. The asking, Daniel was good at. And the answering, God was very good at. But the listening was the hard part. Being able to block everything out—emotions, traditions, status quo, politics—so he could hear. Certainly, if he was going to address this issue of Main Street Bar and all the noise that came with it the right way, he needed extra wisdom. And not of the natural sort.

"I have to stay faithful to what the Word says without pushing people away," he said to his wife. "I mean, you know as well as I do, it's complicated. Some churches have no problem at all with drinking. Others interpret the Scriptures to forbid it without exception, and they preach people to Hell over one drop." He scooted the straight-backed wooden chair away from the table and faced her.

"I know, sweetie."

"I know it's not for me—and it's definitely best to abstain—but I can't remember ever preaching *against* drinking." Daniel sighed. "I guess . . . well, I guess I don't like talking about it in general." Marsha gave him a sympathetic, knowing smile. She was the only person alive that knew exactly what alcohol had cost him.

"I've never felt like I needed to preach on it, not with our congregation," he went on. "And now, people being so upset about Main Street Bar . . . It just feels like a distraction from more important things."

---

1   James 1:5

"It will all work out. And God will give you wisdom, honey," she said. "All you have to do is ask Him. You know that."

A rush of excitement caught in his chest. "Did you see my lesson notes for tonight? *Just now?* Do you know what I'm teaching on?"

Marsha looked at him curiously. "No, why?"

"What you said—about getting wisdom from God—that's *exactly* what I'm studying right now." Maybe it was a sign.

She flashed a toothy smile back at him. "See there," she said. "He's speaking already."

Just as pretty as she was in college, maybe prettier, Marsha now carried sophistication and womanliness along with her beauty. And her faith was unshakable. She was his rock when it all got to be too much. All four-foot-nine of her. As solid as they came.

Marsha leaned against the kitchen counter, enjoying her beverage. "Think about it this way," she said. Her voice was high-pitched and cute with a less-than-subtle Southernness. "You know that 'all things work together for good.'[2] With this new . . . um . . . establishment might come a new harvest. New stores of any kind bring new money to town; and new money means new people; and new people mean souls. And souls need Jesus."

It was a matter-of-fact way of looking at things, but she was right. Boy, did she know how to get his attention. Nothing motivated him more than a chance to spread the Gospel. *And* she'd confirmed Speedy's suggestion.

"I think I should start by going to meet the owner," Daniel said. "I'll just invite him to church and see what happens. Sure, it seems

---

2  Romans 8:28

improbable. But who am I to limit God?" He slapped his hands on the table as a sense of purpose rose up. "I'll go tomorrow."

Marsha gave him a sweet smile and nodded.

"But,"—his wide eyes narrowed with a new thought—"I can't very well just waltz into a bar, now can I?"

She tightened the lid on the bottle and returned it to the fridge.

"Well, you could, dear," she said, "but if you ask me, it sounds like the start of a bad joke."

Her tiny mouth turned up on one side at her own cleverness.

"Oh," he said and chuckled, waving a hand in her direction. "I'm serious now."

"I know. And don't worry about it." She turned around and set about emptying the dishwasher. "I'll give my brother a call. I'm sure he can arrange an introduction. Richard has no qualms about going in there."

\* \* \*

Daniel grabbed his keys, and Marsha picked up her purse from the end table near the door. Bible study was supposed to start in twenty minutes. Daniel had one foot across the threshold when his cell phone rang from the pocket of his dress shirt. Marsha looked back and rolled her eyes as she smiled. She always gave him grief about the dueling banjos ringtone.

He answered as he closed the door behind him and headed for the gray Camry in the driveway.

"Daniel, I'll keep this short," the voice on the other end said. "You and I both have services to lead soon."

It was Reginald Carson, the pastor of the church closest to Springville Community Christian, as the crow flies. His church, Solid

Rock Worship Center, was similar in size and in doctrine, and Pastor Carson had been there even longer than Daniel had pastored SCCC.

"Nice to hear from you, Reggie."

Daniel winced. The perfectly normal greeting was a fib. They were in a hurry, and he had a suspicion the call would not be pleasant, so it really *wasn't* nice to hear from him. Not today. And not when he needed to stay focused on the message he was about to deliver.

"Brother Whitefield, I saw Clifford Goins this afternoon."

A response of "And?" or "What's your point?" felt entirely appropriate, but Daniel refrained.

"I have to tell you," Pastor Carson continued, "I was disappointed to hear that you've chosen not to join our group. Now, we've known each other for a long time, and I'm trying to give you the benefit of the doubt."

"Um . . . " Daniel was so dumbfounded at the accusation that words escaped him. "I . . . "

"Though I have to wonder how your congregation feels about your decision."

They reached the car, and Daniel switched the call to Bluetooth so Marsha could hear. She would help keep him in check if his temper flared.

"Uh, Reggie, I think you're a bit confused. I've not been invited to join any group. Or did I miss something?"

"I believe the invitation was implied." His tone was like the business end of an overly-sharpened No. 2 pencil. "You're a Springville pastor, so you should join up with the Springville League of Churches to make a formal statement about a bar opening up right in downtown Springville. It only makes sense."

"Oh, I see." He was glib. "Well, since I'm on my way to church, I'll just talk to the congregation and see how they feel about me not joining."

Marsha shot him a look. It said to dial back the sarcasm.

Reginald cleared his throat like he was preparing to unleash.

"So, it's true then? You're not against this establishment? I'm surprised at you, Daniel."

Pastor Carson was roughly twenty years older than him, and his stern voice reminded Daniel of being scolded by his father so many years ago. Daniel softened his tone, respectfully, but without apology.

"I'm against it in the sense that I'm not for it," Daniel said. "I wish it weren't happening. There are many businesses that would be more profitable to the town, socially and spiritually speaking. But with all due respect, Pastor Carson, I think your group is unnecessary." He breathed in deeply as he backed out of the driveway. He couldn't be late for service.

Marsha reached over and squeezed his free hand, bolstering his confidence.

"What I mean is," Daniel continued, "if you feel led to do it, then by all means, follow your convictions. I support you. But I just don't feel like I'm supposed to speak out. Not yet."

Daniel had left Pastor Carson nowhere else to go with the argument. He muttered something that sounded like, "Okay, then," and hung up abruptly.

Marsha simply patted his hand and remained quiet while he mulled things over.

Uproar in the town over the bar was bad enough, but adding discord with another pastor—a good man whom Daniel respected—made his heart cry out all the more for answers.

Before bed that night, Daniel took blank notecards from the back of his Bible and wrote on two of them with a permanent marker, as he did whenever he needed to meditate on Scripture. On the first, he wrote the verse from James that had been his sermon text that evening. On the second, he wrote a verse from 1 Corinthians.

*Now I plead with you, brethren, by the name of our Lord Jesus Christ, that you all speak the same thing, and that there be no divisions among you, but that you be perfectly joined together in the same mind and in the same judgment (1 Cor. 1:10).*

No division. But how was it possible?

\* \* \*

It was Thursday morning and still dark outside. Marsha grabbed the cordless phone from the bedside table and handed it to Daniel. Waking on the first ring was a skill they both possessed—a pastoral superpower adapted from years of experience.

He looked at the alarm clock as he said hello. *6:30 a.m.*

"Daniel, I'm sorry to wake you," Reverend Carson said. His deep voice was gruff, but not with malice. His words were garbled up with distress, choked-back tears, and maybe not enough sleep.

"It's okay, Reggie," Daniel said. "What's the matter?"

"I thought you'd want to know. There was an accident last night. Rebecca Truett was killed in a car crash."

"Oh, no."

Cold chills ran down Daniel's arms, and his heart plummeted to the bottom of his stomach. Marsha sat up in bed quickly and leaned in next to him. He turned to look at her. Her eyes said she knew what the call was about, but they pleaded to know who.

"Speedy's granddaughter," Daniel whispered away from the phone. The pained look on his wife's face forced a single tear from the brink of his eyelid. "Rebecca."

Marsha got out of bed and kneeled beside it. As Daniel processed Reggie's words, he watched his wife, on her knees in her cream-colored, silky pajamas. Her lips moved frantically, but no sound came out. She was moving Heaven. Too late for Rebecca, but not for Speedy and his family.

"I'll come over to the hospital right away to see them," Daniel said.

"I'm sure they'd appreciate that. And so do I. Maybe I can tap out for a while."

"Of course. You know I've got your back, Reggie."

"Speedy's been a member of my church for years and years," Pastor Carson said, "but I believe he thinks more highly of you than he does me."

Daniel loved Reggie for trying to ease the blow of the news.

"Do they know how it happened?" It didn't really matter. Sweet Rebecca was gone. But maybe knowing would help make sense of the senseless.

Reggie's breath came out hard and staticky into the phone.

"It was a drunk driver, Daniel. She was on her way home, and . . . the guy who hit her had just left Main Street Bar. Their first weekend open and already this."

"No."

He pictured more of the scene than he wanted to. Against his will and like a bad dream, his imagination played it out. Shrieking tires. The breaking glass and bending metal. Then he saw Rebecca as a little girl, the time his daughter Claire's scout troop held a sleepover at their house. Rebecca and Claire were both in fourth grade at the time. Or maybe fifth. Sometime just before the first signs of womanhood, when they both had braces and giggled at everything whether it was funny or not.

Marsha would be the one to call Claire at college, after her 8:00 a.m. class, and tell her the news. Maybe she'd come home. Maybe she'd drive the three-and-half hours from his alma mater in Greenville so they could grieve together and he could hold her while she cried.

Reggie spoke again, and Daniel was suddenly aware of how long the line had been quiet.

"I'm not tryin' to pour salt, brother, but . . . do you see now why it's so important to speak out against this bar?"

Daniel gripped the phone so hard, his hand hurt. He wanted to throw the receiver, but it was glued to his skin. From some Source other than his own long-cultivated knack for diplomatic banter, he managed to answer, "I hear what you're saying, Reggie." And he hung up the phone as Marsha prayed on.

## Chapter Three

THE AIR WAS COOL, BUT the sun shined brightly onto Main Street.

"Richard, thanks for meeting me down here. I'm sorry I had to cancel on you yesterday," Daniel said. He sighed from a place deep in his soul. "It was a really, really tough day."

His feet marked the cadence of his words as Daniel and Marsha's brother, Richard, walked down the sidewalk, headed from the public parking lot beside the chamber of commerce office toward Main Street Bar a few blocks down.

Daniel had sat with Rebecca's family for hours on Thursday morning. In addition to doling out equal amounts of hugs and tissues, he offered comforting words. He recited the usual verses about not weeping as those who have no hope and about the place God has prepared. He prayed with them and brought them coffee. Wherever there seemed to be a need, he tried to meet it. And it had zapped all his energies, as usual.

Now, the irony of Daniel's current goal didn't escape him. He was on a mission to meet the man that some people felt was responsible for Rebecca's death. No matter. The assignment was clear. Daniel had been given a very specific task, and he intended to carry it out. Piece of cake. Ten minutes tops and he could rest, knowing he'd done his job—inviting Adam Curtis to Springville Community Christian Church.

"I know. And it's no problem, Danny. I'm happy to help my favorite brother-in-law," Richard said. "Even if . . . "

Richard's face was twisted up in a question mark.

"Even if what?"

"Even if I really don't understand why you need a chaperone."

"That's okay, buddy." Daniel slapped him on the back. "You don't have to understand. I appreciate it, anyway."

Between the two, a stranger spotting them on the street would probably peg Richard as the preacher over Daniel. He was known by everyone in town, never without a suit and tie, and nary a hair out of place. But a preacher he wasn't.

"Just promise me you aren't gonna tick him off, okay?" Richard said. His auburn mustache turned up on one side, along with a matching eyebrow.

"You know me better than that," Daniel said with a quarter smile, pretending to be insulted.

"Well, I think I do. When Marsha called me, she said you just wanted me to introduce you to Mr. Curtis. But after what happened with that girl getting killed, I just want to make sure your intentions haven't changed. I mean, I don't think he needs a sermon."

Daniel stopped walking, and so did Richard. They stood in front of the flower shop, and the afternoon sun shone off the dark window at just the right angle to make it look like a mirror instead of plain glass.

"Look, I am devastated about Rebecca Truett's death. I'm devastated by any car crash fatality in Springville. And this one hit really close to home. Just think, it could have been Claire or Katelynn."

Richard and his wife, Diane, had no kids of their own. He had been too preoccupied with making and keeping money to have children. The closest thing they had was Diane's niece, who was about the same age as Claire and Rebecca.

"So, you *are* here to call him out," Richard said. "Take him to task, so to speak."

"No, Richard. I'm not. That's what I'm telling you. The guy who hit Rebecca already had a DUI. He could have gotten just as drunk from a grocery store purchase as he could from whatever Main Street Bar served him. That's not why I'm here."

"Okay," Richard said, with a hint of doubt. They started walking again. "And I *am* sorry about the girl."

"I know."

Three-fourths of the way, their pace slowed. Neither were out of shape, but they weren't exactly in shape either. The last few yards were taken at an easier stride, and Daniel studied the building at the end of the street as they approached. He hadn't stepped foot inside the place in years. Not since way before Smitherman's Department Store closed. But he could still smell the freshly oiled wooden countertops and hear the creak of the stairs. Men's and women's clothing and accessories and cosmetics on the top floor; children's clothing, toys, and housewares in the basement. On one rare day when his father was sober, he had taken Daniel there to buy a treat—a reward for winning the third grade science fair. That was 1975, and Daniel got a scuba outfit for his military man action figure.

He could only imagine what it looked like now, with tables and bar stools instead of clothing racks. Probably televisions, pool tables, dart boards, and taps as well. Only once had he ever visited such a place, years ago in college, so much of his imagining was based on television shows and movies.

"Okay," Daniel said as they neared the door. "I need you to go in and ask Mr. Curtis if I can speak with him out here, please."

"Wait. You want me to bring him out here to talk?" Richard stood with elbows out and his fingertips pressed into his sides, like a teacher who'd just discovered a frog in a student's pocket.

"Yes."

"Isn't that a little rude, Daniel?"

"Maybe. But I'd like to speak to him, and I can't do it in there."

Had he not been completely secure in his convictions, Richard's condescending stare might have made Daniel cower. But he stood tall, waiting for his brother-in-law to comply.

"It's like this," Daniel said. "If someone were in trouble and needed help, of course I'd go in. If someone needed to get an important message to someone and there was nobody else to do it, of course, I'd go in. It's not about the building. But if I don't have to, I'm not going to let anybody see me go in that bar. It's called living above reproach, Richard."

They stood on the bottom two steps that led to the walkway of the building. Daniel pointed emphatically at the door. Richard leaned against one of the black metal railings that stood on both sides of the narrow steps.

"You know," Richard said, sighing. He'd dropped his professional-sounding business voice and let the foothills of the Blue Ridge Mountains slip into his speech. "I once heard tell of this farmer preacher. The vet said to give his cow beer for some kind of sickness . . . I don't remember what." He waved the detail away. "But do you know what he did instead?"

Daniel only grinned. He knew the story but let Richard tell it.

"He let that cow die. Wouldn't even let someone buy it for him." He shook his head. "Of all the . . . " He trailed off, disgusted.

"Well, for me—" Daniel paused, tilted his head toward heaven, and squinted, thinking—"for me, it would be like what Jesus said, about the ox falling into a ditch on the Sabbath. But I don't guess it's really up to us to judge that preacher's convictions. Is it?"

Richard shook his head and sighed again, then he rolled his eyes. "A phone call would have worked," he muttered. He turned, climbed the steps, and went up the walkway and into Main Street Bar.

Daniel waited with his back to the business, watching people and cars passing on Main Street, Springville, North Carolina—the place of his birth. Quaint and inviting, the town was like a Norman Rockwell painting come to life. He spied The Soda Shop down the street—the only business original to the space, the only one to survive the building of the highway which directed most traffic away from downtown years ago. Though the businesses were new, the memories were old. Rows of flat-roofed, brick-front buildings, most adjoined. And the sidewalks were the same where they stood every year and watched Springville's grand Fourth of July parade. Indeed, he was blessed with a good little corner of a rapidly changing world.

Beyond the downtown was just *town*. Not midtown or uptown. Just town, with the chain grocery, fast food, and the handful of discount stores, plus the old houses with sidewalks out front. The rest of Springville was rolling country, with a church about every half-mile of winding road and more cows than anyone could count. The country is where he and Marsha lived on a three-acre plot in the house that had once belonged to his mother.

Richard startled him from his contemplation.

"Daniel, I'd like for you to meet Adam Curtis."

Daniel spun around to face Richard and the man he'd brought from inside. His heart did a somersault, and his mouth instantly felt full of cotton balls. The man in front of him looked as if he'd seen a ghost, and Daniel knew their expressions matched.

"Curtis? Is that you?" Daniel asked.

"Danny W.? No way!" Curtis placed a hand on the top of the step rail, as if to steady himself. Neither man moved from his spot.

Richard's eyebrows were raised and his mouth slightly agape as he looked from Daniel to the bar owner and back again.

"Adam Curtis. I can't believe it." Daniel shook his head. "Curtis. Adam Curtis. We always called you by your last name. It just didn't register when I saw it in the paper."

The man was thin and tall with unnaturally tan skin for early March. He was handsome in a rich-looking sort of way; but if the pinstripe suit, Italian leather shoes, and gold chain bracelet were gone, his face wouldn't have made up the difference.

"Some of my business associates call me Curtis, so I answer to both. Say, um . . . I remembered this was your hometown, Danny, but . . . I didn't know you came back here after school."

"You remembered?" Daniel tilted his head in surprise. "Yeah, I came back and got married right after college. Started a small accounting business."

"Married to Marsha," Curtis said dryly.

Daniel shoved his hands in his pockets and cocked his head to the side again.

"Yes, to Marsha."

"You know,"—Curtis waved a finger in the air—"I believe I told you, the next time I saw you, I'd knock you flat on the ground for stealing my girlfriend."

Curtis stepped down, and it took the grace of God and all the gumption Daniel had to not step backward. But Richard, across from him, coward that he was, did step back. He wouldn't join a confrontation unless there was money involved, not even for his brother-in-law.

"Yeah, I remember, Curtis," Daniel said. "You definitely weren't happy with me the last time we saw each other."

Curtis's green eyes narrowed. His jaw was set forward, and his chest puffed out.

Daniel willed his feet not to move. He'd never, ever be the first to throw a punch, but he surely wasn't running away either.

Curtis stepped down again, the toes of his expensive-looking shoes less than twelve inches from the front of Daniel's Hush Puppies. Then Curtis stuck out his hand.

"But that was over thirty years ago, wasn't it?" he said with a smile.

Daniel shook his hand firmly, hoping his relief wasn't noticeable.

"Wait." Richard spoke up from the safe zone. "You guys went to East Carolina together? And my sister dumped you to go out with Daniel? Well, small world, isn't it?"

Daniel jumped in to smooth over Richard's words.

"Hey, you were always quite the ladies' man. I'm sure you found someone else, right, Curtis? Got married. *Right?*"

"Oh, yeah, yeah. Sure. Three times, actually. And that third one lasted a whole five years. Finally got free of her in September."

There was no way for Daniel to respond.

"But enough about me anyway," Curtis said. "How is Marsha?"

"She is good. Great, actually. She was a teacher for a number of years, and then she stayed home with our daughter for a while. Then she worked as a substitute teacher. Still does every now and then. But she helps me out with the church a great deal. She heads our Ladies' Ministry League. They do a lot of good work in the community."

"Right, right. You're a preacher. That's what Mr. Gambill here told me." He pointed toward Richard. "Hard to believe you and Marsha run a church. Especially Marsha. She was quite the party animal back in the day."

Daniel clenched his teeth and forced a smile. *He's trying to get to me*, he thought. It wouldn't work. He knew better about his wife, and the suggestion was laughable.

*Love suffers long* and *is kind . . . is not provoked.*[3]

Daniel looked at Richard, whose face was screwed up in confusion and disbelief; then he repeated the verse in his mind again.

"We've both changed a lot since those days. We have God to thank for that."

Curtis nodded, but his smug face said he was doing Daniel a favor by not challenging the answer.

"So, are you like those preachers who came here yesterday, threatening to have me put out of business? To tell me how evil I am?"

Curtis put on a cheesy smile and threw a fake one-two punch at Daniel's arm.

---

3    1 Corinthians 13:4-5

"No, Curtis. Actually, I came to invite you to church. Only, I didn't know it was you I'd be inviting." He mustered another smile. "If I'd known it was you, I would have come sooner."

Daniel meant every word, but the rest of it—the spiel he could recite in his sleep about service times, outreach opportunities, and special events—wouldn't come out.

"That's nice," Curtis said. "Do you have a card or something?"

Daniel retrieved his wallet from his back pocket and took out a card with his phone number and church information. He handed it to Curtis, who put it in the breast pocket of his jacket without looking at it.

"Well, I would offer to buy you a drink, catch up on old times, but, uh . . . " Curtis snickered.

Daniel looked up and down the street again. He shoved his hands in the pockets of his khaki slacks and rocked back and forth on his heels.

"Hey, that's okay, Curtis," Daniel said. "Actually, I'd like to buy you a drink instead."

*Chapter Four*

"WELL, ISN'T THIS JUST LIKE something out of a movie?" Curtis said as they walked into The Soda Shop. They were greeted by the tinny ring of the bell above the door and the smell of what Daniel thought must be the world's best hotdog chili.

Daniel bristled at the sarcasm and condescension in Curtis's Connecticut accent, but he talked himself down.

*Great peace have those who love Your law, And nothing causes them to stumble.*[4]

The pair took a seat at the bar that ran half the length of the room. As soon as their backsides had touched the turquoise stools that were built into the bar, a short, shriveled-up lady with a barely there, gray ponytail came to get their order.

"Large chocolate milkshake for me, Marge," Daniel said.

"You got it, Preacher." Marge's voice was friendly, though it sounded like how sandpaper felt. Turning to Curtis she said, "And what about you, honey?"

"I'll have the same, but skim milk in the shake, please. Unless you have almond milk, in which case, I'll take that."

Marge's raised eyebrows peeked through thick, bluntly cut bangs. She stared at Curtis as if he were from another planet, then pushed

---

4   Psalm 119:165

the glasses up higher on the bridge of her nose and walked away. She took two foam cups from a tall stack beside the freezer, then set about making the milkshakes, leaning her whole body in to scoop the ice cream from the bottom of the container. The soles of her tennis shoes dangled two inches from the floor, and Daniel tensed at the possibility of having to pull her out of the freezer like he'd done one time last summer.

"So, you didn't go back home after college, huh? Bridgeport, was it?" Daniel asked. Small talk about anything other than Marsha and him was the objective.

"Yeah, I did for a little while. But there was just something about this part of the country that drew me back." He paused with a thoughtful expression on his face that quickly gave way to a smirk. "Oh, yeah. I know what it was. Money." He laughed, a greasy chuckle that made Daniel's stomach turn, despite his intention to see the best in Curtis.

"I landed a great job with a real estate developer in Charlotte and made more money my first year than my father made in five years as a cop back home."

"Good for you," Daniel said, and part of him meant it. There was nothing wrong with being ambitious and making a good living, but the look in his eyes when he talked about wealth told the story—Curtis's soul and his wallet were inextricably connected.

Marge shuffled toward them carrying a milkshake in each hand.

"Okay, here's a full-fat, chocolate shake for you." She set the cup in front of Daniel. "And a slightly less-fattening, chocolate shake for Mr. Hollywood here." She placed the second cup in front of Curtis, then walked to the other end of the bar and started wiping it down.

"So, how did you wind up managing bars?" He was careful to say it without judgement in his voice.

"Oh, I don't manage them. I own them. And several other businesses. Restaurants. Apartments. I'll be heading out of town once the manager I've hired gets the place up and running well."

"Oh, I see, I see. But why *here*? Why not a big city with lots of people?"

"Two reasons. The space was perfect, and it was cheap—too cheap to turn down. Even though I had to wait six months for the town council to approve the zoning. Bunch of uptight windbags."

Curtis picked up the milkshake and, holding the straw to one side, threw it back like a pint.

"Thankfully, that brother-in-law of yours finally helped me wear them down."

Daniel tried to hide his surprise, but Curtis must have read it on his face. His smirk said so.

"It's not exactly a metropolitan, but if I give people a place to come relax and hang out with their friends, and if I give 'em good booze at a decent price, they'll come," Curtis said. "You know, I wish you could see what I've done with the place. It looks amazing."

Daniel sipped the milkshake at an imprudent pace. Halfway down, the shiny cherry sank beneath the chocolatey surface.

"But you wouldn't step foot in there, would you? 'Cause you think it's a sin, huh?" His tone was mocking. "You and those other preachers. A whole herd of them caused a real scene outside of my bar, you know."

"Well, for *me*, it is a sin," Daniel said. His words were calm and measured. "I'm pretty certain of that, based on Scripture. I'll admit that, for others, it may not be exactly black and white. But I look at it this way: Not everything that isn't sin is good for you. The apostle Paul said, 'All things are lawful for me, but not all things are helpful.'"[5] He moved his gaze from the creamy liquid in the bottom of his cup and looked at Curtis. "I know there are lots of different opinions about it around town, and some people are louder than others. But when it comes down to it, Curtis, I think we're all trying to follow God the way we think we should and look out for our town."

Curtis was quiet, and his brow was furrowed. Daniel sensed he should keep going. Whether it actually changed anything or not, he had a chance to help his old classmate understand his viewpoint, as well as the environment.

"And it's not just about what the Bible says, though that should be at the top of everybody's list of reasons. But in Springville, it's also about holdin' on to something. Preserving who we are. I don't mean to sound prideful, but—"

"Of course not. That is one of the seven deadlies, right?" Curtis interrupted.

Daniel ignored him.

"We have something special here in Springville. I mean, we're not Mayberry, but in some ways, it still feels like it did back then. Everybody lookin' out for one another and takin' care of each other. Things are simpler here than most other places, and havin' that shaken up, even a little, is . . . well, it's unnerving to people. Curtis, no matter how tame your place might be, some people hear *bar*, and all they can think of is rabble-rousers, and debauchery, and the degradation of an entire town."

"Look, I'm not out to destroy Mayberry."

---

5    1 Corinthians 10:23a

"I know that, Curtis." Daniel took a long slurp of the milkshake. "And I don't think you could if you wanted to. It's not like people around here don't drink. There's plenty who do. We're world-famous for the old moonshine runners. And now we've become the Napa Valley of the East in these parts. There's a least twenty wineries within a fifty-mile radius. Who knew that after the factories closed down, this Carolina soil would be put to use growing grapes? But think about it. Those wineries aren't in the heart of the town. They aren't in the building where people used to take their children to line up to see Santa Claus every year. They aren't in the place where mamas found the perfect Easter dress for their little girls and little boys were fitted for Sunday shoes."

"Oh, don't get all sappy on me now."

"I'm just trying to help you understand, it goes even deeper than theology."

They stayed quiet for a while, with nothing in common to bridge the silence. It was a lifetime ago since the two had been roommates. A Northerner and a Southerner, a nonbeliever and a believer—though Daniel didn't discuss his faith much back then. Both were business majors; both were kids figuring out how to be adults, who both fell for the same girl. Despite Daniel's receding hairline and the little wrinkles that had secured their territory around his eyes, and despite Curtis's fake tan and the trying-too-hard highlights in his hair, Daniel still saw in the mirrored wall behind the bar the twenty-year-olds they once were. Those kids had shared a tiny living space for two semesters. Now, sitting here at the counter, neither spoke of it.

"So, why *weren't* you with that bunch that came yesterday? You won't come into my bar, but you didn't stand out there preaching in front of it either."

"I just don't feel it's the right approach. Not for me."

"But you *are* against me?"

"I'm not against *you* at all. But if people are getting drunk in your bar, like the guy that killed Rebecca Truett, then yes, I'm against it. I have to be. I just don't think it's up to me to try to shut you down."

"Danny, I hate what happened to that girl," Curtis said, "but you can't blame me. I was there that night, and I saw the kid that hit her. He seemed fine when he left."

"Well, I feel sorry for him. Matthew, I think his name is." Daniel let out a long sigh. "I can only imagine the kind of guilt he's carrying."

Curtis snorted. "Wait . . . you feel sorry for the sinner?"

"First off, we're all sinners. But this kid has to live with the consequences of his choices for the rest of his life. Look, I understand that plenty of people go to your bar and leave perfectly sober. And I know plenty of others are at least responsible and arrange for a driver if they're gonna need one. But I believe you have a responsibility to make sure you aren't serving people too much alcohol, then letting them leave with car keys in hand."

The bell above the door sounded again as new patrons arrived. Curtis looked over his shoulder, then scanned the room. He lowered his voice to a whisper.

"I'll be honest with you, Danny. But this is just between you and me." He pointed a threatening finger Daniel's way. "That's one thing I didn't think through completely with this little venture. Mayberry doesn't have a single taxi service, and as far as I know, only one drive share service. Except for that, the closest ones are thirty miles away. Technically, it's not my problem. But I'm not completely heartless."

Daniel held his breath, as an idea bubbled up from his spirit and landed in his brain. What some might have called an *aha* moment, and perhaps even crazy and impetuous, was clearly a heavenly road sign. He was sure of it. He wasn't supposed to speak out against the bar. He was supposed to minister to its patrons. The devil hadn't given him an obstacle. God had given him a mission field.

"What if we could work together somehow?" Daniel said. "To get people home safe."

"What are you talking about? You want me to *pray* them all home safely? That's the business you're in, isn't it?"

"No, I could drive them. And I think I could recruit some help."

"So, if someone has too much to drink in my bar and they don't have a ride, you want me to call the preacher? Ha. There's got to be a catch here somewhere. A punchline."

"*Why?*" Daniel spun on the stool to face Curtis. "Think about it. If I stand and scream out against the bar and all the preachers cause enough trouble that you have to shut down, people are still gonna go out drinking. They're just gonna go out of town, and that's even more dangerous. But *maybe* by making myself available to drive someone home, we can prevent accidents."

Daniel may not have painted the complete picture, but it didn't matter. Curtis wouldn't understand, anyway.

"All right, Danny W. If you say so, I won't turn you down."

Daniel raised his nearly empty cup toward Curtis.

*Of course, you won't. We're following a plan.*

# Chapter Five

"I CAN'T BELIEVE ADAM CURTIS is in Springville."

Marsha sat in the armchair of their cozy living room in their simple, ranch-style house with her short legs stretched out and her feet propped on a small footstool. Her soft, brown eyes were round as she listened to the story.

"You can imagine *my* surprise," Daniel said. He leaned back against the couch, grateful for the welcoming softness of it. "It took me a moment to place his face, and then another second to be able to speak. Of all the people . . . "

The both of them being home on a Friday afternoon, alone, still felt strange, but in a good way. This new life season—with Claire gone and with Daniel no longer working two jobs—was like breathing a new kind of air.

"And he actually mentioned *me?*" Marsha asked.

"You can ask Richard. Curtis said right there in front of him that I stole his girlfriend."

"Oh, Daniel." Marsha rose from her seat and joined him on the couch. "You know it was never like that. We hung out a couple of times at parties. And we had dinner together once—before that night I met you. I don't even like to think about those times."

"I know, sweetheart. But he was obviously very smitten with you. And when you and I started dating and got serious so fast, he thought I betrayed our friendship. But how could I blame him for wanting you to be his?" He stroked her porcelain cheek. "That's what I wanted from the moment I first saw you."

She laid her head on his shoulder, and he breathed in the scent of her lavender shampoo.

"You didn't steal me away from anybody. I was always yours. I just didn't know it until I saw you at Curtis's birthday dinner."

"I was just glad it was right before graduation. It would have been pretty awkward to keep sharing a room with the guy when he wanted to kill me."

"Yeah, and I think my daddy wanted to kill *me* when I came home talking about marrying a guy I had just started dating."

"Seems like a lifetime ago, doesn't it?"

"And only yesterday," she said.

"God had a plan there, sweetheart, and I think He has a plan here."

Daniel looked over at the framed photos on the mantle, evidence of the good plan God had worked in their lives. Along with their wedding photo were pictures of Claire—her first birthday, her baptism, junior prom, and high school graduation. The mantle was a timeline of happy occasions. He let his mind wander, imagining what kinds of photos might be added down the line.

Their tortoiseshell tabby jumped onto the couch from the floor, tiptoed across Marsha's lap, and nestled in the small space between them.

"Hey, Chewy," Daniel whispered as he petted the animal's soft fur. He redirected his attention to Marsha. "So, you're okay with my idea?"

"How could I not be?" She took over petting Chewy. "It wasn't really yours to begin with, was it? My only question is, *how long*? Do you know how long this project will go on? I mean, are you sure it's just a project? It seems more like you're taking on another job."

"I know it seems like an open-ended thing." Daniel shook his head. "But I just have this peace that we'll accomplish whatever purpose He has—a specific purpose—then He'll show us when it's time to quit. I can't ask the men to do this indefinitely. But maybe they'll be willing to see what comes of it."

"Well, I'll be there ridin' shotgun if you need me. Whenever you want."

She reached up and mussed his hair.

"I know you will, sweetheart." He looked into her kind eyes, and they drew a contented sigh from his chest. "People are probably going to think I've lost my mind, you know," he said. "Of all the unusual assignments I've been given, I think this is the strangest. Definitely the most unexpected."

She laughed. "Well, if it works out, maybe you *could* take on a part-time job as a regular driver. Work for that new company everybody keeps talking about in big cities." She reached over to put her left hand on top of his, so that their wedding bands touched. "Listen, sweetie. Some people won't understand what you've decided to do. And they may think you're crazy. But it's okay. I'm sure people thought Peter was a little strange when he went lookin' for coins in a fish's mouth. And Moses, when he hit a rock with a stick to get water. And the disciples probably got some strange looks when they started handin' out five loaves and two fish among five thousand people. But you work with what the Lord gives you."

He reached across and put his free hand on top of hers. Could there have been a more perfect helpmate than Marsha, Daniel didn't know how.

Chewy wriggled from beneath their combined arms and jumped down.

"If there's any trouble, I already know who's likely to cause it," Daniel said.

He restrained from calling names. There was no need. She'd been right there with him in the trenches all these years. It was her flock, too, in a way. They had agreeable ones—the vast majority—and not-so-agreeable ones, all with their own good intentions.

"I know what's really got you worried," she said, "and I know you don't like to talk about it. But this is different, honey."

She was right. He didn't like to talk about. It was something he'd rather forget. Even after all these years, it plagued him. The first outreach of his pastoral career had been a failure, plain and simple. Maybe a different group of volunteers would have worked. After all, preaching on the streets in the nearest big city wasn't a *bad* thing. But one man and a group of women on the wrong corner late at night had caused suspicion, and the only person they ministered to that night was the policeman who stopped to talk to them.

The faux pas had been hard to keep quiet. One member in particular had never let him live it down and acted like it gave her the right to question everything the church did—from bake sales to mission trips.

"That was a long time ago, and your listening skills are better now," Marsha said, pointing a finger skyward. "This will be fine. Yes, it's unorthodox. But Jesus's teaching was pretty unorthodox in His day."

"You're right, dear. I have to forget about the past. And who knows? Maybe through this ministry, I'll be able to reach Curtis, too." Daniel rubbed a hand across his tired face. "I'd like to think he's forgiven me. He was friendly enough when we parted ways. But I got this weird vibe from him. Like he was still a little upset." He patted her leg and chuckled. "Let's just pray he's not plotting some kind of twisted revenge for me stealing you away."

"Oh, don't talk like that," she said.

"I'm only kidding."

Daniel gently and reluctantly eased from beneath Marsha's cuddle and stood. He hitched up his slacks by the waist and drew a deep breath. "I guess I need to go make a few phone calls, see if the men are up for an early morning meeting. We've got work to do."

## Chapter Six

"MEN, THANK YOU FOR GIVING up your Saturday morning, especially on such short notice. And I apologize about the accommodations."

Daniel surveyed his troops, all crammed into the smallest Sunday school room in the basement of Springville Community Christian Church. Posters of illustrated Bible scenes adorned the bright yellow walls, and an attendance roster with rows of tiny stickers hung on the door.

Saturday morning was a busy time. The choir was rehearsing in the sanctuary. The Ladies' Ministry League, which Marsha led, was putting a fresh coat of paint on the walls of the other Sunday school rooms, having started with the smallest room first to test out the color. And the fellowship hall was being decorated for a baby shower.

"I called you because I need a favor," Daniel said, "and you are the ones I feel I can count on to help me. You are dependable, faithful members of our church, men of integrity and a heart for the Gospel. Plus, you all have cars."

The men exchanged curious looks. The six of them, ranging in age from twenty-five to seventy-five, had no notion about why they were there. All Daniel had said on the phone was that he wanted to talk about a special project. Yet they came without question—two deacons and four lay members.

The men sat in metal folding chairs—some at the short, rectangle table in the middle of the room and some against the wall. Daniel stood in front of them and whispered a silent prayer that he'd assembled the right group.

"As most of you probably know, I have a funeral to attend this afternoon. A friend of my daughter was killed."

He looked at the floor and choked back tears as he thought of Claire. Her grief was powerful, compounded by the fact that she couldn't come home for the funeral. Too many obligations at school. Daniel wanted so badly to be able to hold her and comfort her.

"Harvey, I think you're going to the funeral, too. Is that right?" Daniel said as he looked up again.

Harvey Hill nodded. He and his wife were both retired. They lived close to the diner and were frequent patrons and long-time friends of Speedy's.

"Well, that funeral has a lot to do with why I called us together. Rebecca Truett's death could have been prevented," Daniel said. "If Main Street Bar had not served a young man too much alcohol and if anyone had been there to drive him home, Rebecca's family would still have her with them. Nevertheless, we understand God is sovereign, and He has a purpose, even in death."

"Pastor Whitefield, why don't we join up with the League of Churches to get the bar shut down? I hear they've organized church members to stand outside at a certain time on Friday and Saturday nights to pray." Alex Martinez was only twenty-five but already a fierce prayer warrior. The son of hard-working parents, Alex was preparing to take over the family plumbing business, but he had the most passion in his eyes when he spoke about working for the Lord.

"That's good to hear, Alex. Certainly, prayer vigils are good. And I'm glad the League of Churches has shifted their focus. I don't think it started out quite so peacefully."

"No, it didn't," Harvey said. "I was at my daughter's store down the street when they first confronted the owner. I could hear them from inside the store, yellin' and carryin' on." He spoke matter-of-factly. "I don't mean to judge, but it didn't seem fittin' at all."

"I know what you mean, Harvey," Daniel said. "And I hope you all can understand why I don't feel led for us to join this group. I respect their intentions—very much. And I respect the pastors. Many are dear friends. But I feel like God has a separate purpose for us, and I feel it very strongly."

"If God has spoken to you, I want to help with whatever He says do," Nikolas Kostas said in his thick, Greek accent. The newest member of the congregation, the owner of the barber shop downtown, had a big smile and eager eyes, like Alex's.

Daniel smiled back. The men were responding the way he'd hoped they would.

"What do you think we should do?" The question came from Greg Thomas, a tall, fair-skinned man with sandy hair. He was a middle school teacher who had attended SCCC all his life and was the one Daniel was most concerned might turn him down. Greg was practically still on his honeymoon. After only four weeks of marriage, he might not be excited about leaving his bride.

"Well, I'll get right to it," Daniel said. "I want a team of men to be drivers, to pick people up from Main Street Bar and take them home if they need it. And before you say anything, you need to know this is about much, much more than keeping drunk drivers off our roads.

That's important, for sure. And it's the reason I mentioned Rebecca. But we're also talking about eternity, the salvation of souls."

There was an awkward silence, followed by a couple of heavy sighs as the weight of the mission settled over the room. Some men looked down at the floor and others at the ceiling, but no one looked at the pastor. He welcomed the pause. Surely, God was working in their hearts. Their heads just needed time to catch up.

In the quiet of the room, a faint refrain of "Where He Leads Me" came from the choir through the floor of the sanctuary above them.

"So, you want us to be like *taxi drivers?*" Stewart Bruce's voice was small, and he looked down at the table while he spoke. Stewart was a middle-aged man who lived with his mother in a little house close to the church. People constantly swapped his first and last names by mistake, but he was too timid to correct them. Despite his meekness, Stewart was a smart businessman and had taken over Daniel's accounting business when he decided to retire.

"Pretty much, Stewart. But not for fares. On a donation basis. Because it's a ministry, we won't charge—but also because we don't have a business license or insurance. As long as we're doing it for free, we should be clear of the legal stuff, as long as you all have personal insurance."

Some of the men nodded right away in understanding.

"Now, for the record, I don't want this mission to be about preaching to people about alcohol consumption. It's bigger than that." Daniel took a seat at the end of the table. "Not everybody, but some people . . . they only drink to cover up their hurts. Like my father did. He drank away the pain of his childhood. And that's the type of people we should ask God to send us. The most broken. The ones who use it as a numbing agent for life. Those are the ones we can show there's a better Way."

He studied their faces. If only he could read their thoughts. He'd prayed hard about the group to assemble. These were his first-round picks. But if any of them said no, he wouldn't blame them.

"We'll have a captive audience. To witness." Alex's face lit up as he caught the vision. "They may not be the most attentive, but the Word won't return void."

"You've got it, my man," Daniel said. His hands met in a clap.

He went on to tell them about his meeting with Adam Curtis, and they wore looks of surprise when he shared that the two had been college roommates.

"Now, there's still a lot of this to work out. I'm going to need your help with the details—if you're willing to join me," Daniel said. He looked to each one individually, tilting his head down and raising his eyebrows in a question mark. As he went around the room, some spoke; some only nodded; but all six men responded affirmatively.

"All right!" Daniel said, as an unexpected lump formed in his throat. It was like watching Claire get her first hit at Little League or walking across the stage to get her high school diploma. Even the ones much older than he were like his children—his brothers, yes, but also his children. And they were making a good choice to graduate into bigger things.

The men looked around at each other, smiling and nodding with the same sense of comradery as a football team huddling before a play. Alex and Greg high-fived, and Harvey and Nikolas shook hands.

"Okay," Daniel said as he sat down with a notebook and pencil, "let's talk details. I was thinkin' of a one night-per-week schedule,"

Daniel said. "There are seven of us, and we can each take a night. I doubt we'll even go out much. We may not even get one call for weeks. But we'll be available, just in case. Sunday through Thursday, maybe until eleven? We don't have to be out *too* late during the week. Then on the weekend, I'll take Friday and can be on-call until one." Saying it out loud, the plan didn't seem quite as crazy as it had when he'd rehearsed it. "But somebody else will need to take the other long shift on Saturday night, unless we want to split it up. And we can rotate days if you want, to make it fair."

As Daniel had hoped and expected, Alex's hand shot up. "I'll take Saturdays. It's no problem," he said.

Daniel smiled at the young man and nodded his thanks. "Now, what else do we need to think about?" He drummed the eraser of his pencil on the notebook. "There's got to be more."

Greg raised his hand timidly. "Um . . . I can't have another woman in my car, especially at night."

"No, of course not. You're right." He pointed at Greg with the pencil. "None of us can. Not without cameras. We'll have to invest in some kind of dashboard camera. And they'll have to be on at all times for our own safety. Sometimes, living above reproach means being able to prove it."

"Won't that be pricey, Pastor?" Harvey said.

"Maybe. I haven't looked into yet. But we won't ask the church for the money. How about we use any donations we get to pay for them? I'll cover the cost upfront; then the ministry can sort of pay for itself."

"Sounds good to me," Nikolas said. The other men nodded.

Since Friday and Saturday were already covered, they worked out the other days among them, and Daniel wrote all the days in his notebook:

*Sunday—Harvey*
*Monday—Greg*
*Tuesday—Nikolas*
*Wednesday—Homer*
*Thursday—Stewart*
*Friday—Daniel*
*Saturday—Alex*

"Pastor, if you want to get started right away and not wait on the cameras, my wife can ride along with me tomorrow night. If we get a call, that is." Harvey was as eager as the rest of them. "Would that be okay?"

"I think that's a great idea," Daniel said. "If Curtis calls me to say someone needs a ride tomorrow night, I'll call you. And Greg, you're welcome to take Trisha along Monday, too, if we happen to get a call and she wants to go." Greg's eyes lit up.

"And another thing," Daniel said. "I'd like for us to keep a journal of the rides we give. A log of some sort. It can be as simple or as detailed as you want. But if we document names and addresses, we can send them a letter later on, inviting them to church. And maybe documenting the ministry will be a good way for us to see and tell about what God's doing with it."

"Now, what shall we call our band of merry men?" Nikolas asked, leaning forward with a wide smile on his olive face.

"Yeah. The ladies' group has a name. I think we need an official title like the Ladies' Ministry League has," Stewart agreed.

"Well, if we start doing lots of projects like they do, I think it would make sense to call ourselves the Men's Ministry League," Greg said.

"I agree," Daniel said. "And maybe this project *will* be the first of many."

"But what about this project? What do we call it?" Nikolas said.

"Living Water Taxi Service," Harvey said. "Or . . . wait, wait. I know." His giant hands hovered over the table. "How about New Wine Transportation Company?"

There were no other suggestions, and all agreed the second of Harvey's ideas was the best. There would be no business cards or grand opening event, no announcement in the paper or flyers to hand out. But New Wine Transportation Company had officially been born there in the littlest Sunday school room of Springville Community Christian Church.

"Homer, you've been quiet so far. What do you have to say about all this?" Daniel said.

The senior statesman of the group, a sometimes farmer and an inconspicuous sage, leaned his chair back on two legs and placed his hands, fingers locked, on top of the Pointer label on the front of his overalls. Full of humble wisdom and quiet authority, Homer Smith was the grandpa everyone wished they had. He spoke softly and slowly, delivering each of his words with care, rather than tossing them out and letting them land any which way.

"Well, you can't very well scream and yell nobody into Heaven. And you can't drag 'em there. They ain't gonna go unless you show

Jesus to 'em. And I reckon' I can do that from behind the wheel of my old, beat-up Dodge as good as I can anywhere else."

The lump in Daniel's throat returned, and all he could say was amen.

*Chapter Seven*

THE GREAT DEBATE WITHIN DANIEL'S heart was whether the details of New Wine Transportation Company should be shared with the congregation or kept quiet. He contemplated it while the choir sang and while the offering was being taken. He mulled it over while the children recited memory verses and during the special singing. And he was no closer to the answer when he stood up in the pulpit than he had been when the ministry was officially started the day before. On one hand, transparency seemed best. On the other, good works were to be done without fanfare.

*Who am I kidding?* Daniel thought. He was *really* afraid of how the parishioners would react. What if they rejected such an unorthodox outreach? What if no one understood his heart for it?

Daniel stepped up to the lectern and looked out at the sea of familiar faces. The morning sun, filtered through stained glass windows, cast a golden glow above their heads. From the elevated platform that ran the width of the sanctuary, he surveyed his flock. Hungry spirits showed through expectant eyes. They came to be fed from the Word, and it was up to him to serve what the Lord had provided. Without distraction.

He casually adjusted his suit jacket and smoothed his tie, whispered a prayer, and began his sermon. It flowed effortlessly, pouring forth like water from a spigot. After his Wednesday night study in the first chapter of James, he'd decided to continue in the book, not realizing that he'd be preaching to himself as much as anyone, from the second chapter. And though he had studied and planned and had written down his key points, halfway through the oration, he stopped even trying to look at his notes. He allowed God to speak instead, and the words became new to him. Fresh. Purposeful.

"'Faith without works is dead.'[6] But we don't work for the Lord because we have to. We work for the Lord—we serve others—because the Spirit compels us to be servants like Him. It's not works that save you; but if you have faith in the Lord, that will be evidenced by your obedience to Him when He gives you a job to do. Especially the hard tasks like He gave to Abraham, as we see in verse twenty-one."

For the duration of his sermon, he had supernatural focus. He saw, but was unfazed by, the few crying infants, fidgeting toddlers, and snoozing seniors. But near the end of the service, during prayer requests, his concentration waned, and the great debate recommenced. Maybe he should ask the congregation to pray for their new mission. Or casually mention it as a closing announcement.

Daniel opened his mouth, but a lady in the back spoke up first.

"I'd like for y'all to remember my mama. She's been in the hospital for a week with a bad flare-up of colitis."

"Yes, let's keep Mrs. Thurgood in our prayers," Daniel said solemnly. He gripped both sides of the wooden lectern and looked down and back up again slowly. Then he froze.

To the woman's right, at the end of the pew on the back row closest to the door was Adam Curtis. Had he been there the entire service?

---

6  James 2:26

Any thought Daniel had of announcing the new ministry to the congregation flew right out the stained glass window. His throat was suddenly dry, and there was an uneasiness in his chest that he didn't understand. Daniel quickly called on a deacon to close the service with prayer; and while heads were bowed, he walked to the back as he did every week, ready to greet people on their way out of the church. He pretended not to see Curtis as he passed.

People soon began filing out, and Daniel tried to greet them as normal. He smiled and asked how they were feeling, and he accepted compliments on the sermon. But he kept a watch on the line, looking for Curtis. He'd been in the back. Something must be keeping him.

Sincere, but distracted, he spoke to each one who came by.

"Yes, Mr. Jennings, it is a beautiful day today."

"I'm glad you're feeling better, Wanda."

"Clarice, thank you for praying for me. I could feel them up there today."

Finally, he saw Marsha nudging her way through the crowd, and she came to stand alongside him, as she often did.

She leaned in close and whispered like a ventriloquist. "Adam Curtis is here."

He gave her a nod that said he already knew, keeping his this-is-the-day-the-Lord-has-made smile on his face, though his insides were shaking—yet another pastoral superpower.

"How are you, Mary Jane?" Daniel spoke to a heavy-set woman, who had a passel of small children playing all around her and squeezing through her stockinged calves. She seemed to pay no attention to them as she talked to Daniel about the hardship of their father being deployed again.

Marsha bent down to talk to one of the children, and Daniel caught a glimpse as the pigtail-haired little one showed her a picture she had drawn of him during service with his Bible raised up over his head. "This is such a good picture," Marsha said. It was a fine likeness, indeed, even if it was in crayon.

As he listened to Mary Jane's troubles, interjecting a sympathetic *uh-huh* every now and then, Daniel admired his wife from the corner of his eye. The little girl's eyes beamed up at Marsha as if she were an angel. To Daniel, she was.

Marsha was great with children. If they had been able, they would have had a brood like Mary Jane, who—except for the little girl with the pretty picture—were now all playing leap frog in the vestibule. But it wasn't just children. Marsha made everyone feel loved and welcomed, just like being home. Her eyes invited conversation. They seemed to say, "Talk to me. I'm just like you."

As Mary Jane gathered the children to leave, the pastor and his wife directed their attentions back to the remaining procession; then Marsha squeezed Daniel's arm. They'd let down their guard, and their old friend seemed to have snuck up on them, popped into line unexpectedly, just like he'd shown up in Springville. Curtis was dodgy, like the moles that tunneled under their front yard and popped in and out from strategic holes all around. Those devils tormented Chewy.

"Curtis," Daniel said pleasantly. "I'm surprised to see you here."

"You did invite me, *didn't you?*" Curtis said. "I think it's rude to turn down a sincere invitation. Plus,"—he turned to Marsha with a look of admiration so obvious that it made Daniel's skin crawl—"I wanted to be able to congratulate Mrs. Whitefield on the wedding. Though, I guess I'm a few years late, aren't I?"

"Hello, Curtis," Marsha said. "It's nice to see you again." She spoke as politely as she would to any other visitor; but she linked her dainty arm with Daniel's, and her forearm muscles tensed next to his as she gripped him.

Curtis reached as if to shake Marsha's free hand; but when she offered it, he swallowed it up between both of his and held it there instead, even while she held onto her husband with the other. Curtis's eyes were fixed on hers, and thirty years of wondering and wishing for what might have been poured out of them. Could the line of parishioners behind Curtis see it, too?

Marsha attempted to gently pull her hand away. Daniel felt the subtle flinch from her. But Curtis's gold-ringed fingers pressed more tightly into her fragile ones. He seemed to take pleasure in making them both uncomfortable.

Some folks left the line, nodding at Daniel as they passed. The line had been stalled for some time. Still, many waited patiently for their weekly audience with the pastor.

"Remember, Curtis, um . . . I'll have my phone on tonight," Daniel said, hoping to distract him. "Have the manager call me if anyone needs a ride. I've got someone on standby to drive."

Curtis nodded but didn't look away from Marsha, and he didn't release her.

At just the moment Daniel was ready to put a stop to it by whatever means necessary, Agnes Reynolds stepped up to the trio, and the brashness of her entry made Curtis turn and let go of Marsha's hand.

"So, it's true," she said. It was a statement, not a question. A statement punctuated by extreme displeasure in her shrill voice. "You're really starting a taxi service for drunks under the name of Springville Community Christian Church."

For such a short, round woman, her presence was formidable—enough so to make Curtis bow out of his power game. He winked at Marsha, nodded at Daniel, and left them there to face Agnes—a long-time parishioner with a one-of-a-kind knack for giving Daniel heartburn. She was always the first to point out flaws and the last to try to make things better. And Daniel gave thanks daily that there was only one such challenge in his congregation. He loved her as a Christian sister and respected her as an elder, but as he had often told Marsha—because God knew what was in his heart anyway—he wouldn't be sad if one day she made good on her threat to leave SCCC and go to Reggie Carson's church instead.

"How do you think this looks to the people of Springville? Think about appearances, Daniel," Agnes said.

"I have, Agnes. And I agree. We do need to be mindful of appearances. But I'm more concerned about my appearance before God. I'm concerned with doing what He tells me to do." He covered up his aggravation and annoyance masterfully with an even tone.

"Well, I think it's like handin' a bank robber a gun. You're enablin' sin by doing this."

"Or saving a life, Agnes," Marsha interjected calmly. When it came to dealing with women, Marsha was better equipped. God had blessed her with an extra measure of patience.

"We agree that it's sinful to be drunk," Marsha said reassuringly. "But this is an opportunity to witness. Part of the Great Commission."

Marsha's logic fell on deaf ears.

"I voted for your husband to get a raise," Agnes said. She hoisted a heavy-looking purse onto her sloped shoulder. "After serving our congregation for so long, he deserved it. And now, especially after he's quit his other job, I don't want any reason to question my vote."

At least she'd had the grace to keep her voice down.

Marsha reached a calming hand across to Daniel and pressed it into his chest. The weight of it said, "Let it go. It's okay." And when neither of them responded to Agnes, she waddled away with a huff.

*First Curtis, now Agnes Reynolds.* Daniel felt like running to his car with Marsha and heading home as fast as he could before anyone else decided to ruin his day.

Most of the remaining congregants had given up and headed out the door as well. Waiting wasn't worth the risk of missing the diner's lunch buffet. But Harvey and his wife, Colleen, stayed, and Colleen wore a shocked expression that told them she'd heard everything. She took Daniel's hand in hers.

"Don't listen to her, Pastor," Colleen said. "We have faith in you. I believe you're following the Lord's direction. It doesn't matter what Agnes thinks. God has a purpose in everything. Besides, she has no business talkin', not with the way she depends on her homemade *cough medicine.* All it takes is a tickle in her throat, and she's reachin' for the top shelf." Colleen closed her eyes for a second and pursed her lips backward. "I'm sorry, Pastor Daniel. That wasn't kind."

"That's okay, Colleen." Daniel smiled. She always meant well. And weren't they all works in progress?

Colleen moved on to hug Marsha, and Harvey, coming behind her, shook Daniel's hand, too.

"You must be doing something right, Daniel. You already got the owner of the bar to come to church. That was him, wasn't it?" Harvey said.

"Um . . . yeah. That *was* him. Caught me by surprise, for sure."

"See there. God must be workin'. Try not to worry about Agnes. And by the way, that was a wonderful sermon you gave."

His most faithful deacon had tried to make him feel better, but Daniel, still shell-shocked, could only nod.

"I'm excited about my first shift," Harvey said. "I don't know if we'll get any calls, but I have a really good feeling about this. There's no telling who we'll get to help and how."

Despite the encouraging words, Daniel couldn't think about the ministry for long. His mind quickly went back to Agnes and her attitude and to Curtis's big, sweaty hands and how much he never wanted to see another man look at his wife that way again.

# Chapter Eight

New Wine Transportation Company, Driver Log
Date: Sunday, March 10
Drivers: Harvey and Colleen Hill
Passenger: Rita (Last Name Unknown)

THE CALL CAME AT 9:30 p.m.

"Oh, this feels like an adventure," Colleen said as she climbed into the passenger seat of their SUV. Harvey was already buckled and ready to go. He agreed, but didn't say so. He kept his excitement pushed down, just under the surface, though he gripped the steering wheel hard and drove just a little faster than normal.

As they drove the short distance to Main Street Bar, Harvey imagined who might be waiting for them. They were breaking new ground as the first volunteers. It was uncharted territory. And Daniel had called with only one piece of information: Someone named Rita needed a ride home.

There was no manual for how to start a church-sponsored designated driver team because, surely, such a thing had never been done. But Harvey had a Word from the Lord, and that was all the instruction he needed for the night. "By this all will know that you are My disciples, if you have love for one another."[7]

---

7    John 13:35

She was waiting out front when they got there, sitting on a bench near the door. Her hand was palm-down beside her, and she propped herself on a long, slender arm. The thin, spaghetti strap dress wasn't right for the cold night air, and she had no coat. At least her legs were covered with dark leggings and tall boots.

There were few places to park near the entrance, so Harvey left the SUV in the street with the flashers on and with Colleen waiting inside.

The girl looked down at the sidewalk as he approached her slowly. He cleared his throat as not to startle her, but she jumped anyway. Maybe Colleen should have come with him. It wasn't very well-lit in front of the bar, and Harvey had an intimidating frame.

"Are you Rita?" he asked softly.

The girl nodded, and the way she looked at Harvey made him think of a little, lost lamb.

"I . . . um . . . I heard you need a ride? I'm Harvey Hill."

"You're a driver? With like, a taxi service?" she asked. Her voice was shaky.

"Yes. I work for New Wine Transportation. We're a new venture," he said. "My wife is in the car. She'll be riding with us wherever you want to go."

Rita stood, and Harvey studied her. She seemed steady enough. He walked toward the street and let her follow him. He walked slowly, without turning around, and only picked up the pace as they approached the car, so he could open her door.

"Miss?" He presented her chariot with a sweep of the hand.

She pushed her shoulder-length, strawberry-colored hair behind an ear and looked up and down the street; then she took one step forward and paused again. A light mist began to fall, and Rita reached a hand to cover one of her mostly bare shoulders.

Colleen, in the front seat, looked back and called to Rita.

"Hey there, sweetie! Get on in and get yourself warmed up."

Rita crawled into the backseat obediently.

As Harvey put on his seatbelt, he gave Colleen a quick, wide-eyed glance, and her expression answered him. Rita couldn't be very much older than their granddaughter, Grace—a freshman in high school.

"Where to?" Harvey asked.

"What? Oh, um . . . "

The girl was dazed, but certainly not from alcohol. He couldn't smell any at all.

She stared out her window, leaving Harvey's question unanswered. He waited until they got to the next stoplight on Main Street before he asked again.

"Where would you like to go, Rita?"

The girl skipped right past misty, teary-eyed, and weepy and broke straight into an I-can't-breathe kind of sob. "I don't know," she wailed.

Colleen turned around in her seat to face Rita, shifting her hips for a better view of the girl's face.

"What's wrong, honey? Are you okay? What do you mean you don't know?"

"I don't know where my car is."

Harvey steered the SUV into the empty parking lot of a bank and stopped. He turned around to look at Rita, too, and they both waited quietly while she composed herself.

"I met up with this guy at a friend's house," Rita said. "Then he asked me to follow him to his house. I did, and we rode to the bar together, but . . . but . . . he left with some other girl and left me there by myself."

"Okay, dear," Harvey said. "Don't cry. We'll figure this out."

Colleen reached into her purse and pulled out a small pack of tissues. She handed them to Rita, who took them gratefully.

"So, let me make sure I understand," Colleen said. "You need to get to your car, but you're not sure how to get to where it is."

Rita nodded.

"I can't go home without my car. My dad will kill me! And my mom will be so disappointed. I shouldn't have gone with someone I don't know. And I don't want them to find out where I went."

"Well, I think we can help you. And as far as your parents . . . they might be upset, but I bet they'll mostly just be happy you're okay," Colleen said. "We all make mistakes, sweetheart."

Rita stopped crying and wiped the mascara off her zebra-striped cheeks with the tissue.

"Okay, now think," Harvey said gently. "Do you remember what his house was near? What did you see while you were driving?"

Rita blinked the watery haze away from her blue eyes.

"It was really close to the water tower."

"Okay, I'll head that way; then we'll figure out where to go from there," Harvey said.

"Are you warm enough now, sugar?" Colleen asked as they pulled out of the parking lot.

"Yes, ma'am," Rita said. "Thank you both for being so nice. I feel like I know you. Like I've seen you before."

"Probably around Springville," Colleen said. "Maybe at the diner?"

"Maybe."

"Or you might have seen my wife on television," Harvey said.

"Wait!" Rita slapped the leather car seat. "You're the lady who went on that game show! And you won some money."

"It was second place, but I did get a little money—and some very nice parting gifts," Colleen said.

If people hadn't seen Colleen's episode of *Risk and Reward* with Rodney Vaughn that aired in January, they'd seen coverage of it in the *Springville Chronicle* or on the local news channel. It wasn't just a television debut that people were excited about or the fact that she'd walked away with a nice chunk of change. It was that Rodney Vaughn himself had called her the most charming contestant he'd ever had on the show, without a hint of exaggeration in his Hollywood voice.

"That's so cool. I wish I could tell my mom I met you. But I don't want to have to tell her I had to get a ride home."

"Darlin', how old are you?" Colleen said it like someone who had a right to ask.

"Seventeen."

From the rearview mirror, Harvey saw Rita hang her head. He looked at his wife, who wore the same furrowed brow.

"So, how did you get into the bar?" Harvey said.

"I didn't order anything. I promise. The guy I was with only gave me a tiny sip of his beer, but that was all."

"And nobody asked you for I.D.?"

"No, sir."

Colleen and Harvey exchanged another concerned look.

"Well, there's the water tower, just there," Harvey said. He pointed out his window to the gray bucket in the sky. "Look around. Can you remember where you went from here? There's the old textile mill there." Harvey pointed the opposite direction of the water tower.

"Is that what that empty building is? I never knew," Rita said.

"Yep. My daddy worked there all his life," Harvey said.

"And it's the reason my family came to Springville when I was a little girl," Colleen said.

"Okay, here's some houses." Harvey continued to scan the landscape, describing them to help jog her memory. "See, just over there is a little neighborhood with lots of short streets that cross one another like a plaid shirt, but on the other side is a long, dead-end road with a handful of houses on it. Look familiar?"

There were no other cars to be seen, and Harvey drove at a snail's pace as Rita looked from one window to the other.

"It was only one turn off this road, I think, but I can't remember which way."

"No worries. There aren't too many options. We'll just try them all until we've found the right one." Harvey smiled at her in the mirror.

"I can't believe y'all are being so nice to me."

"Well, why wouldn't we? You seem like a nice girl," Colleen said.

Harvey turned down the dead-end street first, following a hunch. Three houses down, on the left, Rita spotted her car in the stranger's driveway.

"That's it! There's my car. Thank you! Thank you! Thank you!"

Harvey parked on the unmarked street.

"Now, where is it that you live, Miss Rita? We'd like to follow you home to make sure you get there safely, if that's okay."

She nodded with a wide smile that said she was glad to be looked after until she was back where she knew she should be.

"I live out on Sycamore Road." She reached into her tiny, black purse. "All I have is five dollars. Will that be enough?"

"Honey, you keep your money. We were happy as we could be to do it," Colleen said.

Rita said nothing, but she started to cry again.

"Here, take this," Harvey said. He handed her a church card, along with a tissue from the box in the console. "We'd love to see you again."

She rubbed her finger over the fine cardboard and stared at it for a moment, then looked up again with the most curious expression on her face, as a single tear ran down her cheek. There was no more mascara to smudge.

"Thank you," she whispered, and she got out of the car with keys in hand, springing out like a deer and darting to the car.

They followed her Jetta for about fifteen minutes to Sycamore Road. The front porch light was on. Someone was waiting for her. And Harvey said a prayer in his heart that all would be well for Rita.

As he headed for home, Harvey was overwhelmed with satisfaction, the kind one gets after completing a job and doing it well. There had been no mention of God and His overwhelming love. There had been no chiding over a teenager's foolish decisions. But they had shown her Jesus. And Harvey trusted that He could take it from there.

The clock on the dash read 10:25. Surely, Daniel hadn't gone to bed already. It was worth the risk. Harvey had to tell him what a success their first call had been.

Daniel answered the phone sounding wide awake.

"Hey, Harvey. How did it go? I've been praying for you."

"Pastor, it was great—"

"Here, let me talk to him, sweetheart. You're driving." Colleen leaned over and took the phone. Without any greeting, she proceeded to tell him all about Rita and her predicament and how grateful she had been for their help. When she'd gotten all the happy news out of her system, she handed the phone back to Harvey.

"Brother Daniel, I think we're definitely doing what we're supposed to be doing. And that's what it's all about, isn't it?"

Daniel agreed, and they hung up the phone. In their excitement, they'd failed to tell him the troubling thing—Rita's young age and the fact that she'd been able to even get into Main Street Bar. There'd be time for that later. Maybe when they met again on Saturday, he'd mention it.

When the couple arrived home, Harvey stayed in the car for an extra minute by himself. First, he said a prayer for Rita. Then he took a moment to scribble down a note on the driver log notepad.

*Log Notes: Helped a little, lost lamb find her way home tonight. Sweet girl. Praying we see her in church one day. Underage drinking at Main Street Bar could be a problem.*

## Chapter Nine

BY MID-MORNING ON MONDAY, DANIEL had driven an hour away to buy the cameras—a straight shot on the highway—then back again. He'd found them on sale, the kind that mounted to the dash with suction cups so they could be moved between cars. Instead of dropping the money on one for each of the men, he bought three. And when the manager of the store found out what they were for, he gave Daniel an employee discount, bringing the total to right around a hundred dollars.

By 11:00 am, he had delivered one of the cameras to Greg's house and one to Nikolas at the shop. Daniel decided against a haircut, for the sake of time, but it took him thirty minutes to get out of there, anyway. Nikolas and his customers were chatty.

After the barber shop, it was off to Homer's house to deliver the third camera. As he drove up the dusty driveway, he could see his elderly friend milling about in the old shed. Not much bigger than a child's playhouse, Homer's shed was piled to the roof with junk.

Homer turned around as Daniel's car approached, and he waved to him with a broad smile on his face.

"I hope I'm not botherin' you, dropping in like this," Daniel said as he got out of the car.

"Oh, no, preacher. No bother. I's just lookin' for something to tinker with."

"Well, you're in luck. I brought you something." Daniel held up the boxed dashboard camera.

Homer's face lit up. "All righty then! Let's get to it."

Homer led Daniel to the carport and stood, studying two cars parked underneath, then he turned and faced two other cars, rustier ones, parked behind the shed. Turning back again, he held his chin in his hand and looked back and forth at the vehicles in the carport.

"I reckon' this one would be better than my truck," Homer said. He pointed to a white Nissan sedan, probably early nineties.

"As long as it runs, it'll work just fine, Homer." Daniel patted him on the back. "Let me install this, and then I'll show you how to turn it on."

Homer stood outside the car as Daniel worked.

"You know, I'm kind of lookin' forward to my turn," he said.

"Uh-huh? I'm glad to hear it." Daniel stifled a tickle in his nose. The inside of the car was dusty.

"I know we're supposed to be tryin' to reach the lost," Homer said, "but it's kind of excitin'. Like somethin' out of a movie or a program on TV. Never done nothin' like it before."

Daniel leaned his head out of the door and smiled up at Homer. "I guess I can see that. It *is* pretty exciting."

The installation was finished quickly, and Daniel showed Homer which button on the camera would start the recording. Easy enough. To show his gratitude, Homer invited him to stay and have a piece of rhubarb pie. Daniel checked his watch. There were other stops to make—and rhubarb pie wasn't his favorite—but he couldn't turn down such a sincere invitation.

Homer's wife, Rachel, seemed overjoyed to serve him.

"It's not too sweet, is it?" she asked.

"No, ma'am. Just right," Daniel said, after he swallowed his first bite.

The three ate together at the little table on the screened-in back porch, since the sun had come out and brought a little warmth with it.

The porch was long and narrow, with old bottles and crates and other things Homer liked to hang on to stacked in the corners.

"I canned the rhubarb last year. It came out of our garden," Rachel said.

Homer smiled at his wife proudly. "Our pantry is stocked plumb full, thanks to her canning skills."

"That's wonderful," Daniel said, smiling. He scraped up the last bit of syrup from the plate and licked the fork clean. Rhubarb pie was better than he remembered.

"I taught Gwen how to make this pie when she was living with us. First time I've made one since she left."

Rachel's frail hand covered her mouth as the tears formed in her eyes.

"There, there, honey." Homer reached over and placed a hand on her arm. "It's all right now."

"You still haven't heard anything?" Daniel asked.

"Six months. Not a word."

"I'm so sorry, Homer. I'll keep praying."

Daniel knew what a toll their loss had taken. Their granddaughter had lived with them since she was fifteen. Now in her early twenties and a drug addict, she seemed to have disappeared from the face of the Earth.

He checked his watch again. He was supposed to be somewhere else, yet he was exactly where he needed to be.

"Why don't we pray for her right now?" Daniel said.

They held hands around the tiny table, their empty pie plates in the middle, and petitioned the Father on Gwen's behalf.

\* \* \*

By late afternoon, Daniel had visited three patients at the hospital—one heart case and one mother and new baby. Then he'd gone to the church to meet the insurance adjuster on account of some minor roof damage from a late winter storm. The good news was that the deductible was less than Daniel thought it would be.

Now he sat in his driveway with the car off. No radio, no cell phone. There was less than an eighth of a tank of gas left in the car he'd just filled up three days ago, and he was running on fumes himself. He stared at the house. That sagging rain gutter needed attention, but he couldn't even muster the energy to get out of the car. His legs wouldn't work. They were tree trunks, and his body was perfectly conformed to the car seat.

There was still plenty of daylight at 5:30 p.m, and he was grateful. The start of Daylight Savings Time and the budding crocuses at the end of the driveway both told him that spring was coming. It wouldn't be long. The dark days of winter were over, and new life would soon burst forth. If they could just make it through this last month of winds and cold snaps, then warmth would be theirs for nearly the next seven months.

Daniel's exhaustion, coupled with the start of a headache just above his eyebrows, kept him behind the wheel. Of course, he had a headache. All he'd had to eat that day was a piece of rhubarb pie. He leaned back against the headrest and closed his eyes, so relaxed that his mouth opened the span of a fifty cent piece and stayed that way. Marsha was out shopping and wouldn't be home until close to dinnertime. Maybe he'd just sit there until her blue Mazda pulled up beside him. Hopefully, she wouldn't think he was dead.

His eyes became weighted like sandbags, and a gentle tingle flowed from head to toe before he didn't know anything anymore.

* * *

Daniel jerked upright at the *tap, tap* of knuckles against glass. A familiar face floated an inch from the window.

"Are you okay, Daniel?" Reggie Carson said.

He looked to the other side of the car. Marsha still wasn't home. He looked in his rearview mirror to see Reverend Carson's Suburban parked behind him. The sky was now the color of ash. He checked his watch. Only a twenty-five-minute nap, but he felt like Rip Van Winkle.

Daniel nodded and opened the car door. He got out slowly, blinking away the sleep as he stood.

"Hey, Reggie," Daniel said. "You caught me in a little cat nap, I guess." He rubbed at his eyes.

"Busy day, huh?"

"Yeah, yeah. Pretty busy." What all had he done? His head was still cloudy with sleep. "Come on inside the house," Daniel said.

He fumbled for his keys.

Once inside the house, Reggie took off his long trench coat and hat and laid them across the burgundy armchair. The men sat down on opposite ends of the couch, like they'd done on more than one occasion. Chewy came in, sniffed around at the guest, then settled in on the arm of the couch beside Daniel.

"Daniel, I'll get straight to it. I came by to see if you've given any more thought to joining the coalition," Reggie said. "Your church is an important part of this community, and we'd like for you to stand with us."

Reggie smiled like a used car salesman. His full, gray eyebrows contrasted against his dark skin, raised in anticipation of Daniel's yes.

"But . . ."

"Now, I know you've already spoken your piece, but as your friend, I'd like to encourage you to reconsider."

"Reggie, I—"

"I've always admired your resolve. You're a man of integrity, and I believe you and I share the same views on Main Street Bar. It's no good for Springville."

It wouldn't be an easy argument. Reggie was a bulldog after a bone. Daniel twisted the heels of his hands into his temples, then pulled his hands down the length of his face. He reached for his Bible on the end table and slipped out the card with the verse he'd written a few nights ago. *No division.* He took a deep breath.

"And what exactly is your group doing?" Daniel asked. The least he could do was give Reggie a chance.

"Well, the prayer vigils mainly. And we plan to petition the town council. Maybe even hold a rally at the next council meeting. But if nothing else, just having a unified front shows the community we won't accept the moral decline of our town. We don't take it lightly."

"And what do you think the town council is going to do?" Daniel asked. "They can't close it down. And they can't take back the zoning permit. It's just not logical."

Reggie bristled. "Maybe it's because this Mr. Curtis is a friend of yours. Is that it? Is that why you're on his side?"

Nothing was kept quiet in Springville. Nothing.

"Look, we were roommates in college, but that doesn't make him my friend. As a matter of fact, he's pretty much the opposite. But even if he was, it wouldn't change my view."

Reggie sighed. "Well, there has to be a reason you are so against joining with us. I hate to ask, but are you planning to make a little extra money with this taxi business I hear you've started? Is that why you don't want the bar shut down? I mean, I didn't think you'd need to moonlight to make ends meet."

A slap in the face would have hurt less. Daniel fought to remind himself that Reggie was his friend. He was a good man who, in his frustration, said some nasty things.

"Reggie, that's not true. We're not out to make money. That's flat-out ridiculous." Daniel kept an even tone.

"Then what *is* it about?"

Daniel was wide awake now. His muscles clenched, and he leaned forward, looking Reggie in the eye.

"Let me tell you something," he said. "I'm as straight-laced as they come, and I've never had my intentions questioned like this before." He choked back anger and tamped it down with his love for the man sitting across from him. "I am *not* afraid to fight hell head-on and declare war on sin any time," Daniel said. His face was hot, and his heart pounded. "Sometimes, we do that by raising our voices and boycotting. Other times, we do it by just loving sinners. That's what we're doing now. Just loving people. There's no agenda. No hidden motive. I'm just doing what I know the Lord has told us to do, and it doesn't matter if anybody understands it or if they don't."

If Reggie had tried to hide his shame, it didn't work. After a moment of silence, he opened his mouth but stopped at the sound of a car door.

Just a moment later, Marsha was inside. "What a nice surprise!" she said to their guest.

Reggie smiled and nodded, but the tension in the air was palpable. Marsha must have felt it because she kissed Daniel quickly and excused herself, carrying her shopping bags into the kitchen.

Another awkward silence.

Daniel skimmed the verse on the card again.

"*Speak the same thing . . . no divisions among you . . . be perfectly joined together in the same mind and in the same judgment.*"[8]

But Paul had written about matters of doctrine. It wasn't the same. It was okay for them to disagree about the coalition because it wasn't a saving issue. He should have seen it before.

Reggie put his hands on his knees, preparing to stand.

"You've never asked me how I got this scar," Daniel said. Reggie looked at him with curious surprise as Daniel pointed to the two-inch white line that ran vertically just below his left temple. "Maybe you've never noticed."

Reggie relaxed against the couch, listening.

"This was a present from my father when I was eight years old. He was out-of-his-mind drunk when he did it. Came at me with a broken bottle. I never even knew why, other than just that—he was

---

8    1 Corinthians 1:10

out of his mind." He rubbed at the reminder on his skin. "Here I am all these years later, and I can still remember how those stitches felt to my fingertips. And I can remember how much he cried and said he was sorry." He craned his head toward the ceiling, sucked in a breath, and looked down again.

"I'm so sorry, Daniel," Reggie said.

"My mother got us out of there not long after. She tried her best to help him, to make it work. But the addiction was stronger than his love for us."

"I don't know what to say . . ."

"I had the joy of leading my Father to the Lord just two months before he died. He'd drank most of his life away, but God saw fit to save him. Can you believe that? *He saw fit to save him.* And He saw fit to let me be there. That's grace, my friend."

"Indeed."

"Reggie, if anybody hates drunkenness, it's me. What it did to me, my childhood. How it wrecked my mother. But I figured out this much: Alcohol isn't the enemy. It's only one of the enemy's weapons."

Reggie scooted just close enough to lay his hand on Daniel's back.

"I hear you, brother. I hear you."

Too much emotion filled the space between them. The manly thing to do was to change course quickly.

"As far as my *taxi service* for drunks," Daniel said, "last night, one of my deacon's and his wife escorted a seventeen-year-old girl home. She wasn't drunk, but she was somewhere she knew she shouldn't be. And she was scared. And God sent them specifically to her, specifically at the right time." He shook his head in awe of it. "I really don't think we'll get many calls. Maybe one a week." Daniel's hands went into the air and back down again. "I'm actually surprised we had one so soon. But God has people that He wants us to reach, Reggie. And we're ready to do that."

"God is good," Reggie said. He rose from the couch solemnly and picked up his things from the chair. "Daniel, I still believe in our coalition. But I won't question you anymore about not joining. Though it'd be nice to have you."

Daniel smiled and nodded and walked Reggie to the front door. The cat jumped down and followed them.

"I'll be praying for your service," Reggie said. His warm, chocolate brown eyes focused in hard on Daniel. "I mean . . . your *ministry*."

"Thank you, brother. And I'll be praying for yours."

The two men shook hands, and Daniel opened the storm door for his friend. Reggie stepped out onto the stoop and turned around. A strong wind came in, sending Chewy scurrying out of the room.

Reggie pulled his coat tighter and shivered.

"Daniel, do you believe in Divine revelation?" Reggie said as he put on his fedora and held it there.

"Of course. You can't walk with the Lord for as long as I have and not believe in it."

"I don't claim to be a prophet, and I can't tell you what it means; but I have the number seven running over and over in mind, and I feel like it pertains to you somehow."

Daniel felt a chill. Was it the wind or something supernatural at work?

"Number of perfection. Number of days in a week," Reggie said.

"Thank you for sharing," Daniel said nodding. "I don't know what it means, either, but maybe we'll find out." He offered Pastor Carson a smile.

*Number of perfection. Number of days in a week. And also the number of men in New Wine Transportation Company.*

Reggie was almost to his vehicle when he turned around with a second-guessing slowness.

"Um . . . Daniel? I hope your congregation will support you. I mean . . . all of them."

"I think most do," Daniel said confidently.

"Well, I'm hesitant to tell you, but"—Reggie stepped closer to his car and put his hand on the door handle—"Agnes Reynolds called me last night. All wound up," he yelled over the howl of the wind. "I'm sorry to say I agreed with her until our talk today. If she calls again, I'll talk her down. But if it were my congregant, I'd want to know."

"Thank you, Reggie. I appreciate it. I don't like trouble, and I'll do my best to handle the discontent."

Reggie nodded and opened the car door. He eased into the car seat, and Daniel gave him one last wave.

Daniel closed the door and whispered a prayer of thanks that the riff between him and Pastor Carson had been mended and a prayer of protection for his congregation—that they would be guarded from attacks from outside and from within. Surely, not even Agnes, the giant wedge that she was, could split Springville Community Christian Church. He hoped.

# Chapter Ten

New Wine Transportation Company, Driver Log
Date: Monday, March 11
Driver: Greg Thomas
Passenger: T.J. Hupert

HOW GRATEFUL GREG WAS THAT he hadn't brought Trisha along like he'd originally planned. With T.J. in the back of his Ford Taurus, the car was no place for a lady, especially his perfect bride. She was at home in their nice, warm bed, with her pretty face resting on a pile of soft pillows. Right where his princess belonged.

T.J. Hupert was in a slightly less royal state. He smelled like a distillery. From the moment he'd gotten into the car, just past ten o'clock, Greg was baffled at how the man could have been so overserved. What exactly was it? Beer? No, whiskey. No, both.

*Aren't there rules about that kind of thing? It's obvious he's tanked.*

Greg was no prude. He'd partied back in the day—nothing too serious, but enough. He wasn't raised in a teetotalling home, so it didn't have the same wouldn't-be-caught-dead stigma as it did for many in town. He even imbibed on rare occasions—but only in private. On their wedding night, they'd ordered champagne. But even with all his experience, Greg had never seen, or heard, or smelled someone as intoxicated as his passenger. Completely wasted. And to make it worse, Greg and T.J. had a history that Greg preferred to forget. His worst fear about this whole idea—driving someone he knew—had come true, though the unshaven, round-faced man slumped against the window was hardly the star quarterback Greg remembered. He used to be Mr. Has-it-All—popular, good-looking, athletic. Where had that guy gone?

"What's your address, T.J.?" Greg said with an eye roll in his words.

"Walnut Lane," T.J. said. He pushed the words out with obvious effort and a nearly lifeless tongue.

No need to ask the GPS. It was near Greg's grandmother's place, just beyond town limits. Greg used to ride the school bus there in the afternoons, and T.J. took great pleasure in making it the most miserable ride ever, dishing out wedgies and wet willies as often as he got the chance. He'd play keep-away with Greg's lunch box, tossing it to one of his buddies, then spitting in it before he finally gave it back. As they got older, the teasing was less frequent but more hurtful— from a random shove against the lockers to spreading vicious lies that made no one want to be his friend.

Greg felt a twinge of nausea. Was it the smell or the memory?

He turned off of Main Street, heading south. There was little traffic this time of night on a Monday. With any luck, he'd be back home and in bed with his bride in less than half an hour. Just thinking about her, he could smell her coconut lotion and feel the subtle rise and fall of her belly as he lay with his arm across her middle, so comfortable. Oh, why did he have to be with T.J. Hupert now instead? And what kind of guy went out and got drunk on a Monday night? What a loser his former bully had turned out to be.

Maybe he should take the opportunity to thank T.J. After all, he was part of the reason Greg had become a middle school math teacher—to encourage young people, to teach them to have confidence, and to try to protect them from kids like T.J.

"So, you're like a taxi driver or sumfin'?" T.J. asked. He pushed himself off the window and sat up in the middle of the backseat. His head fell backward, and he let out a groan.

"Something like that," Greg said to the rearview mirror. Conversation seemed pointless. He probably wouldn't remember the ride, anyway.

"Joe called ya, huh?" T.J.'s lazy words were directed at the roof of the car.

"Yes, the manager of the bar called and said you needed a ride home."

"Uh-huh."

Greg chuckled, though he felt guilty about it. T.J. and his bobbing head bore a slight resemblance to Otis of Andy Griffith fame.

They'd driven about three miles. About six more to go. He turned on a soft rock station, hoping to block out the sound of T.J. slurping his saliva before it could fall out of his mouth. But when T.J. got excited and started slapping the leather seat to the rhythm of Toto's "Africa," Greg turned it off.

"So, you from 'round here?" T.J. asked. If his words had been notes on a piece of music, they would have been connected by a curved line above or below, denoting the slurs.

*He doesn't even recognize me? What a joke!*

Was it the intoxication, or had Greg really been so insignificant that he left no mark in T.J.'s memory? He ought to pull over and kick him out. Leave him on the side of the road four miles away from his house on a chilly evening.

"Yeah, I'm from around here," he said. Nothing more.

Another two miles passed without words. Greg looked in the rearview mirror again. T.J. hadn't moved for some time, and the spit slurping had stopped. He looked from the man to the road and back again, over and over quickly for about thirty seconds. A feeling of urgency rose up in his chest, and he spoke loudly, trying to rouse him.

"Hey, um . . . yeah, I'm from around here. As a matter of fact, I teach at South Middle."

No movement.

"Hey, T.J.," Greg said even louder. "I said, I teach at South Middle."

T.J. raised his head a notch.

"Huh? Oh, yeah." T.J. let out a belch, and the strong odor of it traveled quickly to the front seat. Greg waved a hand in front of his face to clear the stench.

At least he wasn't dead, but it wouldn't be ideal for T.J. to pass out in Greg's car again either. He might not be so easily awoken the next time. And the last thing Greg wanted was to have to haul T.J.'s sorry drunk butt inside the house. Plus, he didn't know which house on Walnut Lane was his. He had to engage him, keep him awake.

"Do you know where that is?" Greg said.

Of course, he would. Everybody did. It was the one that was built right after Greg and T.J. finished high school.

"*Wassat?*"

"South Middle. Do you know where it is?"

"Oh, um . . . yeah . . . my daughter goes there."

"Cool. What's her name?"

"Amy. No, no. Amber. Amy's the little one."

"Two kids, huh?"

T.J.'s head fell back again. "Uh-huh."

Greg wondered if his little girls would be awake to see their dad in such shape when he got home and to hear him call them by the wrong name.

He and Trisha wanted kids someday. They'd take time and enjoy just being married for a while first. But someday, they'd be parents. Obviously, T.J. had gotten started on parenthood a little early. Wait. He must've been . . . *eighteen?* Somehow, Greg had missed that news. Now he was curious. What must his wife be like? Or maybe he and his daughters' mother weren't together. Maybe they'd never been married. Maybe he didn't see his little girls.

T.J. was motionless again, a worrisome kind of still.

"Hey, T.J., we're almost to Walnut Lane. What's your house number?"

He answered that he didn't remember. Great.

They turned down a little road with a No Outlet sign posted. In about a tenth of a mile, the road became gravel. The two parallel beams of light bounced as the car did and changed path with each turn, piercing through the cloudy darkness. There was plenty of fence line and not many houses, and not much road left either.

"Hey, we're on your road, man. You gotta tell me where you live."

Thankfully, T.J. raised his head.

"Can you tell me which one is yours?" Greg said.

"Which what?"

"Which house?" Greg yelled. His anger was audible now.

"Oh." He seemed to suddenly sober up, at least a little bit. He looked around, scanning both sides of the road. He pointed ahead of them to the left. "That one," he said.

Greg slowed and turned the red sedan onto a dirt driveway that was still mucky from last night's rain. The yard was covered in last season's leaves. A thin dog sauntered in front of the car, squinting at the light, then ducked under a sagging porch.

"No, no. Not this one. The next one. The one with the light on. See?" He leaned forward and pointed across the way to the next house down. The two yards were separated by a row of young crepe myrtles.

T.J.'s tensed frame slumped back onto the seat again, and his slurred words became wistful. "See there? She always leaves the light on. She always waits for me. No matter what."

Greg put the car in reverse. Backing out, the left rear tire hit a pothole that jarred the car and made T.J. curse. Greg pulled into the driveway of the correct house, the one with the light on. There were actually two lights—one on the outside of the house, shining beside the front door and illuminating the path of neatly placed stepping stones to it, and one on the inside, coming from the last window on the left, where someone sat up waiting. On either side of the door, along the front of the house, were perfectly-shaped boxwood shrubs. The yard was well-kept. No leaves, no monkey grass, no starving dog. T.J. must've been doing something right. Greg's own yard was a mess compared to this.

As he jammed the gear shift up to Park, he rejoiced inside that the ordeal was almost over. He'd done his duty, carried out the task as the pastor wanted. Now he'd be free of this chore until the next week, and maybe he'd catch a break then and wouldn't get called out.

"Okay, T.J.," he said as he got out of the car, "let's get you to the door." He didn't expect T.J. to do it on his own. He could barely sit upright.

As soon as Greg opened his door, T.J. leaned out of the car and vomited on the ground, barely missing Greg's shoes. Greg jumped back in disgust and spun around to avoid the sight. He covered his own mouth with the back of his forearm and pinched his eyes closed. It was almost more than he could handle.

*What grown man gets that sloppy drunk?*

He forced himself to turn around and was happy to see that T.J. was already out and standing on the other side of the puddle. Thank goodness he hadn't done it inside the car. Greg would be counting that blessing in his prayers tonight, for sure.

T.J. took a wobbly step toward his house, and Greg reluctantly went to his side, spotting him. Halfway to the house, T.J. stumbled, and Greg quickly grabbed him by the waist, with an arm around his back. He picked up T.J.'s arm and placed it across his shoulders, shuddering at the lingering smell.

They made it; and with nothing left to do for him, Greg propped T.J. against the house beside the front door and knocked on it gently. Making sure the heavyset man was stable and wouldn't fall into the shrubbery, Greg turned to go. As an afterthought, he turned back and took a tiny, brown New Testament—the one he read on his lunch break—from his pocket. He placed it into T.J.'s shirt pocket, where it stuck out, just above a fresh vomit stain. T.J.'s heavy eyelids opened fully as he glanced down at the book, then looked at Greg with the faintest hint of a smile.

Their eyes fixed on one another, T.J.'s brow furrowed. He wiped his mouth with his shirt sleeve. "Thank you, Greg," T.J. said. "You always were a nice guy."

He did remember.

Greg nodded, then turned and walked quickly to the car, trying to squelch the measure of sympathy that stirred within him.

As he started the car, the front door of the house opened. A woman in pajama pants and a long t-shirt, with hair piled on top of her head in a messy bun, stepped out and guided T.J. inside the house.

Relief. His passenger had reached his destination.

Greg would call Pastor Whitefield tomorrow and tell him what an ordeal it had been.

His foot rested heavy on the gas pedal. Maybe Trisha would be awake. Maybe she'd left the light on for him, too. After a few miles, the mixture of yucky smells finally vacated his nostrils, and Greg began to reflect on his first mission with New Wine Transportation Company. He supposed it was worthy. Maybe he'd actually saved someone's life. Maybe even T.J.'s.

Greg made it home, but no lights were on. He took the notebook from the dash and scribbled a quick note.

*Log Notes: I'm glad I was able to get T.J. home safely, but I think he's a lost cause.*

# Chapter Eleven

"REALLY! THE NERVE OF CURTIS to call and invite us to dinner." Marsha's voice bounced from their bathroom to the bedroom. It was an uncharacteristic tantrum. Daniel's normally even-keeled wife was a half-step beyond hornet-mad.

"Who does he think," she yelled until Daniel came into the bedroom to spare her voice, "he is?" She took a pair of small stud earrings from the jewelry box on the oak vanity and put them on with shaky hands. Despite the physical handicap produced by angst, her makeup was pristinely done. She wore this certain shade of mauve lipstick, the color of the roses in the backyard in May, that she only wore on special occasions. The scent of her raspberry crème lotion wafted across the room and caught Daniel's nose. He closed his eyes and inhaled deeply with appreciation.

She stomped back to the closet for her heels.

"I just can't get over it, honey! After the way he acted at church and not letting go of my hand like that. I was so embarrassed."

As she put the second shoe on flamingo-style, she lost her balance, and Daniel was there quickly to catch her by both elbows. How fortuitous. He'd found his chance to help Marsha stop talking about Adam Curtis.

He pulled her close and moved his hands from her elbows to her waist, then he planted a kiss on her unexpectant mouth. It went on until she had to pull away to catch her breath, wearing a smile.

"What was that for?" she asked.

He wiped her lipstick from his mouth with the back of his hand, but his grin remained. "I just wanted to change the subject. That seemed like a good subject to me."

She smiled. "Maybe we can talk about it more later."

"And besides," Daniel said, "I'm not going to let that man ruin an evening out with the most beautiful woman in the world. As far as I'm concerned, for tonight, we've never even met Adam Curtis."

She conceded with a nod.

"Are you almost ready to go? I am getting hungry. And it will take a half hour to get to your mother's and still another twenty to the restaurant."

"Yes, I'm almost ready." She checked her watch. "We'll be right on time to meet Mama." She headed back to the bathroom and reapplied her lipstick.

Their already-planned dinner with Marsha's mother was the perfect excuse for declining Curtis's invitation. He'd called the day before with some spiel about catching up and walking down memory lane. Daniel didn't want him walking anywhere with Marsha, and he didn't feel an ounce of sympathy or regret when he told him they would be otherwise engaged.

"Well, maybe another night, then," he had said. "I'm only in town for another week and a half, and I do hope I get to see more of you . . . and especially your lovely wife." Daniel remembered the last word trailing long like a snake's hiss and how it had made his blood boil. He kept it to himself, though. Marsha had been upset by Curtis enough.

\* \* \*

The pastor and his wife would have been just as happy with burgers and fries at the diner. Blue jeans and sweaters. Comfortable shoes. But Marsha's mother, Jacqueline—who enjoyed finer things but lived on a Social Security budget—had found the monthly dinner date when her son-in-law picked up the bill to be the perfect time to satisfy her craving for prime rib. They were happy to indulge her, but on Daniel's pastor salary, it was an only-once-a-month treat, for sure.

"You look beautiful, dear, but stressed," Jacqueline said to her daughter, less than a minute after they were seated. "Are you okay?" Her eyes narrowed behind clear-framed glasses.

Daniel's brow furrowed, and his head tilted to the side. Marsha *was* stressed, but she hid it well. All smiles and bright eyes. Not a trace of worry on her pretty face. But Jacqueline could sniff out trouble like a hound dog on the hunt.

"I'm fine, Mama," Marsha said.

She placed her hand over her mother's on top of the linen tablecloth.

"Everything's okay with the church?" Jacqueline asked.

"Of course, Mama. Why wouldn't it be?"

The waiter came and filled their water glasses. Daniel sat quietly, watching the exchange.

"No reason." A long pause. "But I did hear that SCCC isn't part of the league of Springville churches speaking out against a certain establishment that opened recently downtown. I hope that's not causing any problem within the congregation."

*Here we go,* Daniel thought. It followed him everywhere he went.

Marsha sighed as she placed the cloth napkin in her lap. She shot Daniel a look that said, *you handle this one.*

"We're not the only one, Jackie," Daniel said. "And we're addressing the situation in our own way."

Jacqueline nodded, seemingly satisfied. But Marsha picked up where Daniel had left off.

"Mother, why does Richard even talk to you about things like that? It's not a big deal, and I don't know why everyone acts as if it is."

Her tone was even and non-accusing, but Jacqueline reacted as if Marsha had gone off the rails.

"Now, calm down, sweetheart. I didn't mean anything by it," Jacqueline said. "It's just that . . . oh look, our food is here."

Just like that, she had the last word, thanks to prime rib cooked to the perfect temperature.

The waiter, with a dark vest and tie and a white apron around his waist, brought the tray of steaming plates their way. A shrimp salad and baked potato for Marsha, a chicken sandwich and sweet potato fries for Daniel, and steak, loaded baked potato, and salad for Jacqueline.

As they bowed their heads and Daniel gave thanks aloud, he offered an extra prayer in his mind—a request, for a peaceful meal.

For the time being, Jackie seemed content to focus most of her energy on the food. In between bites, the conversation turned to pleasant matters—the weather and family, the kind of chatter they normally enjoyed during dinners out.

"How's your steak, Mama?" Marsha asked.

She worked on chewing a bite, then answered, "Oh, it's very good, dear. Thank you." She wiped at her mouth, then put the napkin back in her lap. Head down, she returned to the steak—cutting one bite and eating before cutting another off the huge piece of juicy meat.

As petite as her daughter, only more so on account of late-life shrinking, Jacqueline was a curious sight at the table. She wore a burgundy blazer—always a blazer—with the too-wide sleeves cuffed, causing her to resemble a kid wearing their father's suit coat—a kid sitting down to their father's dinner. It was hard to imagine where the seventy-six-year-old fit all of that food.

Daniel exchanged a look of amusement with his wife as they watched Marsha's mother eat. Then suddenly, Marsha's lopsided grin morphed into a deer-in-headlights expression. Something behind Daniel's back had caused her great distress. He mouthed, *What?*, then turned around before she had time to answer. Adam Curtis was headed for their table.

He had to have followed them. Daniel knew it right away. Whether or not to call him out on it now was a different subject. His mind raced, but he breathed another prayer and put it in check.

*The LORD is on my side; I will not fear. What can man do to me?*[9]

"Well, what a coincidence," Curtis said. "Daniel. Marsha." He nodded at both of them. The large knuckles of his long fingers created a mountain ridge of bone as he gripped the back of the empty wooden chair at their four-top.

Jacqueline looked up and dabbed steak sauce off the corner of her mouth as she smiled.

Daniel and Marsha sat like knots on a log, and Daniel's throat felt like he'd swallowed one.

---

9   Psalm 118:6

"Mrs. Gambill, it's so nice to see you again. But I bet you don't remember me," Curtis said. "It's been quite a while."

He stuck out his hand and reached across the table. He turned her hand over when she offered it, as if he intended to kiss the back of it. Instead, he gave a quick, pretentious half-bow and released her.

"I think I do remember you," she said.

Surely not. Marsha said she and Curtis were never a couple. They couldn't have been serious enough for him to have met her parents.

"You went to college with Marsha, didn't you? Oh, well, and I guess Daniel, too," Jackie said.

Over thirty years ago. How did she know him?

"Yes. You have a terrific memory," Curtis said.

"You mean for someone my age?" Jackie joked.

"No, no. I didn't mean that at all," Curtis said. He played the part of gracious gentleman well.

Daniel and Marsha sat on either side of the empty chair, and Curtis faced Marsha's mother. Daniel prayed she wouldn't invite him to sit down. As it turned out, she didn't. But Curtis sat anyway.

"Didn't we meet at the homecoming game?" Jackie said. She didn't wait for him to answer. "Oh, yes. It was senior year for Marsha, and you were there as her date."

Marsha's face became an Antarctic tundra, except two circles that formed on her cheeks the size and color of beets. Was she embarrassed because she'd been caught?

"I do think it was at the football game. See? All the way back to 1988. A very good memory," Curtis gushed. He directed his attention to Daniel without any explanation as to how he'd happened to run into them there. "So, Danny, the manager at the bar tells me your guys have helped us out already with transportation. The last couple of nights, he said." He folded his arms on the table.

"Yes." Daniel choked down a French fry, along with his annoyance. "We had one call on Sunday and one call last night. I think our arrangement is working out well so far."

"Good. Good. I'll tell Joe to keep sending them your way then. Say, I guess I should be getting back to my business associate over there." He gestured to another part of the dining area, but Daniel didn't see exactly where he meant.

"Mrs. Gambill, it was a pleasure to see you again after all this time."

Jackie smiled sweetly at Curtis and bobbed her head in courteous agreement.

"And Mrs. Whitefield"—he turned to Marsha and leaned in toward her, uncomfortably close—"it's, of course, a pleasure to see you."

Daniel cleared his throat loudly and threw the linen napkin down on the table, ready to stand up, but Curtis got up quickly and dashed off. He must have known he'd crossed the line. Of course, he knew. He was doing it on purpose.

"Is he the owner of the . . . " Jackie started.

"Yes, Mother. That's him."

Disregarding the social graces on which she was normally keen, Marsha put her elbow on the table and rested her head on tented fingertips.

Daniel tried to calm his breathing.

"Well, isn't that interesting," Jackie said, seemingly unaware of the tension in the room.

\* \* \*

Leaving the restaurant, the cold air nearly blew them away. A steady drizzle had begun to fall, so Marsha and her mother ducked back into the lobby, and Daniel sprinted to get the car for them.

He pulled his coat tighter as he made his way across the parking lot. The calendar said spring was a little over a week away, but it seemed more like months. Two degrees lower and the rain would be snow. Nothing in Daniel's world seemed as it should be.

On the drive back to Jackie's condo, she went on and on about how perfectly the steak was cooked and how Daniel and Marsha were really too good to her, how she didn't deserve such thoughtful children.

Daniel and Marsha stayed quiet, except for the occasional uh-huh from Marsha in the backseat.

Marsha handed Daniel the umbrella after he parked the car. She got out and gave her mother a quick hug in the rain before hurrying into the front seat. Daniel walked Jackie to her door, shielding her with the umbrella. He waited for her to unlock it. There was no portico, so he held the umbrella over her and only half of himself.

"Thanks again, Daniel," she said.

"You're welcome, Mama Jacqueline."

"Maybe next time we can try that new restaurant over on Miller Street. I hear they have a fabulous porterhouse."

Daniel smiled and nodded. Of course, she'd want to try the most expensive restaurant in all the surrounding counties. He watched her close the front door; then he jogged back to the car, anxious to get out of the cold. It wasn't much warmer inside the sedan.

Marsha's head leaned against the headrest. She stared blankly at the ceiling.

He held it in until they reached the interstate. "So, you let Curtis meet your parents, huh? You never mentioned that."

"What?"

"A couple of parties and a dinner, huh? You never said anything about a football game." Fully aware of how petty he sounded, Daniel didn't care.

"Daniel, it was nothing. There was nothing to mention."

"Seems like a big deal to me. You didn't introduce me to your parents until we were talking marriage."

"We were talking marriage three weeks after we started dating. Be fair! They came to see me at school, and Curtis was at the game, too, so I introduced them. I don't know how or why my mother remembered him."

"Maybe you two were a little more serious than you've told me? Maybe that's why Curtis gets to you so much now."

"You can't be serious."

"I wish I weren't."

"You actually think I've been dishonest with you?"

He ignored the pain in her voice.

"I don't know what to think. I see the way that man looks at you. Like he knows you the way I do, and it makes me sick to my stomach."

"Daniel Theodore Whitefield."

Dueling banjos interrupted, and Daniel pulled the phone from his coat pocket.

"What is it? I mean . . . I'm sorry. I meant, *hello?*"

How timely. As if he needed yet another reminder of Adam Curtis, it was Joe, the manager of Main Street Bar. Someone needed a ride.

## Chapter Twelve

"HEY, NICK," DANIEL SAID. HE gripped the cell phone. "The manager of the bar just called, and . . . "—he turned his head to breathe out hard away from the phone, then back again—"he said a friend of Mr. Curtis's could use a ride tonight. That's all the details I have. Are you up for it?"

The name left a bad taste in Daniel's mouth. It was so tempting to completely cut ties and not have anything to do with Curtis or his establishment again, except for joining the coalition to try to run him out of Springville.

"Of course, Pastor. Of course. Three nights in a row for our mission." He sounded like he'd just won an all-expenses-paid vacation. "That's wonderful."

"I know it's already pretty late, but . . . "

"It's never too late to be the hands and feet of Jesus, Pastor. I'm on my way."

It was a kick in the stomach. Nikolas was eager to serve. So excited for what God had called them to do. It had been God, hadn't it? He'd been so sure at first, but he'd been wrong before. Still, in case it *was* God, Daniel had to persist. He would have to swallow his pride and somehow reclaim the attitude that Nikolas Kostas had, though it seemed that walking naked and blind-folded on a bed of glass shards across a bridge over the Grand Canyon would be easier.

* * *

New Wine Transportation Company, Driver Log
Date: Tuesday, March 12
Driver: Nikolas Kostas
Passenger: Mr. Steven Gorski

Nikolas's car smelled like a bottle of cologne had been spilled in the backseat. Cologne and too many cigars. But no alcohol.

"This ain't exactly a limo, now, is it?" his passenger said in a thick New York accent.

"I suppose not," Nikolas said. "But it gets me where I need to go. And where can I take you on this rainy evening, my friend?"

He hit the black radio button. The song, on a barely-there volume, was easy listening, gospel style. The instrumentation was mostly acoustic guitar; and the singer could have easily passed for James Taylor, but he sang about Jesus.

"Springville Inn."

"From out of town?"

"What tipped you off?"

Nikolas turned the radio up a tiny bit without answering the man, inviting the soothing words of the song to calm his spirit.

The man in the backseat—a Mr. Steven Gorski—was dressed in a stylish suit, and he carried a briefcase—an odd look for a night of drinking.

"Say, how long 'til we're there, pal?"

"No more than ten minutes. Everywhere in Springville takes ten minutes. Quite different than back home in Patras."

Mr. Gorski checked his watch.

"Hey, so you're from that church, right?"

"Yes, I attend Springville Community Christian Church, sir. It's a wonderful congregation. My family has been so welcomed there."

Mr. Gorski waved his hand. "Yeah, yeah. That's nice. Interesting little service you guys are running. A free taxi."

"Well, something like that, I guess. If you're in town for a while, we'd love to have you join us at church. You'd be most welcome."

"So, I hear your preacher went to college with my business associate, Adam Curtis. Down near the coast."

"Yes, that's what Pastor Whitefield told me."

"Yeah, and that Mrs. Whitefield. He's told me some stories about her." Mr. Gorski laughed.

"So, they were classmates as well?"

"Among other things."

Nikolas's mind went cloudy with confusion. What point was there in Mr. Gorski being terse? An uneasy feeling settled in his chest, and he turned the music up again.

"Curtis said the preacher's wife was a little . . . um . . . shall we say . . . a little less than holy back then, if you know what I mean."

His passenger's meaning became clear. Too clear. Mr. Gorski spouted things that shouldn't be spoken, especially about a woman of God like Marsha Whitefield. Nikolas's hands shook, even as he gripped the wheel. It couldn't be true. Marsha was a picture of virtuousness. A fine role model for his own teenaged daughter. He turned up the radio again.

"I'd rather you not speak that way, sir, about Ms. Marsha. She is a fine lady," Nikolas said.

Mr. Gorski shrugged his shoulders. "Free country, isn't it?"

Discouragement settled over Nikolas's heart. How could he show the love of God to this man, who was so vile? He recited Philippians 4:8 in his mind to block out the continued slander. His responsibility was to focus on things that were true, honest, pure, lovely, of good report, virtuous, and praiseworthy. None of the things Mr. Gorski said fell into those categories.

"I just thought you'd like to know. The whole town should know. Curtis says that preacher's wife has paid him a couple visits over at the hotel since he's been in town. Now he's thinking about *not* heading back to Charlotte anytime soon on account of her."

The best thing Nikolas could do was to say nothing. He turned the radio up loudly, and Gorski laughed the gesture away.

When Nikolas pulled up to the front of the hotel and the man got out of the car, he turned the radio down and lowered his window. "Mr. Gorski," he called forcefully. He waited until he had the man's full attention. Gorski stood three feet from the car window peering down at Nikolas with a smirk on his face, and Nikolas allowed his frustration to spill out in four simple yet passionate words: "I don't believe you."

He rolled up the window and drove away.

The immigrant family hadn't lived in Springville for very long, but there was one thing he understood. It was the same all over the world. There were very few secrets, and bad news traveled fast. He had to tell Daniel before his pastor heard it from someone else. No need to record the experience in the New Wine

Transportation Company driver's log. It was an experience he wouldn't soon forget.

* * *

Daniel ignored the ringing cell phone. He'd done enough talking that night to last the next week, maybe two or three. Now it was time to rest.

He rolled over on the sofa and pulled the blanket closer to his chin. Chewy relocated from on top of his feet to behind his knees.

It was the first time in his married life that he and Marsha had slept under the same roof but in different rooms. He didn't blame her; he'd be mad about the insinuations, too. Still, in the back of his mind, the doubts lingered. What if there had been more to Marsha and Curtis's relationship in college? Would it change anything between them? Maybe there were details she'd forgotten. It had been a very long time ago. Certainly, too long ago to let it bother him now.

A phone rang again, this time the landline. It never stopped. All day, every day, someone needed him. Calling, texting, messaging, stopping by uninvited. The work was endless; he never got to clock out.

No, the only person that could make him answer the phone again tonight was Claire. He checked caller ID, then put the handset back on the cradle. Nikolas could leave a message if it was urgent.

## Chapter Thirteen

"I WANT TO ADDRESS SOMETHING very personal to the congregation, and this is not easy to do."

Daniel stood in front of the small Wednesday evening crowd, squeezing the sides of the lectern as if by the strength of his grip, he might be imbued with an equal measure of courage. His neck hurt from sleeping on the couch, not to mention the general tension that had multiplied each day since the bar had opened and especially since first seeing Adam Curtis five days ago.

Despite the difficult task before him, Daniel found solace in at least one thing—he and Marsha had made up. After Nikolas called that morning and tearfully shared what Mr. Gorski told him about the rumors, Daniel went for a long walk in the woods behind their house. He prayed and cried out to God, then realized himself a fool. He and Marsha were being played. Damaging their marriage was exactly what Curtis and the devil wanted. Marsha was the same faithful helpmate she'd always been; and after he had finally come to that conclusion, she forgave him. Now Daniel was in damage control mode, and Marsha was at home, hiding from the shame of the lies that Adam Curtis and his goons were spreading through town.

"I'm sure some of you already know, but I believe it's best to be completely transparent. You are family to me, and Marsha and I need your support and prayers."

He looked out over the congregation from the raised platform. About twenty-five people sat with eyes fixed intently on him.

"There have been rumors started about my wife, and I hope you all will understand and believe that they are just that. Lies. There is a man in town trying to cause problems, claiming that Marsha has been unfaithful to me." He choked out the words, then closed his eyes and bit down hard on his bottom lip. "I want all of you to know, it is absolutely untrue. There is not even a hint of truth to these rumors, and I think all of you who know Marsha well will believe me. They're ludicrous. But please, if you hear any gossip, come talk to us. We have nothing to hide. Now, can I answer any questions to help put your mind at ease about this whole business?"

Just as Daniel predicted, Agnes Reynolds was the first to stand.

"It was shared at the hair salon this morning that Marsha has been entertaining Mr. Curtis while he's in Springville." The word *entertaining* had never sounded so dirty. "Even *if* it isn't true, I'm afraid this reflects very poorly on our church."

Daniel left the lectern and made his way across the stage, down the three steps to the lower level of the sanctuary. He held himself up on a front row pew.

*If.* How could she say *if* it isn't true? After all Marsha had done for the church. After the years she had dedicated to the service of the Lord. They ought to know her better. She was ten times the woman half of them were. She wouldn't even participate in their gossip, much less have an affair.

His heart pounded as he formulated a response. Then came the harsh reality. Just the night before, he had been tempted to believe the worst about his wife. He'd stopped just short of accusing her, and he knew her better than anybody. He knew she wasn't capable of deceit, yet he'd walked right into the trap. And now he was being baited again. Agnes was not the enemy. He repeated it in his mind. *Agnes is not the enemy.*

"Thank you for letting me know, Agnes," Daniel said. "Please trust that I share your concerns, of course. But I have to tell you, I'm more concerned with reflecting poorly on the Kingdom of God than I am this body of people."

Many heads nodded as Agnes sat back down. The look on her face said she wasn't satisfied with his answer.

"Anyone else have a comment?"

A tall, rugged man sat in the middle of the church. He'd been twitchy the whole time, and there was an anxiousness in his eyes. But he didn't speak out yet. Cat-and-mouse was apparently part of the fun.

Harvey's wife, Colleen, kept her seat, but she called out to the pastor in a reassuring tone.

"Of course, we don't believe any of those tales about Ms. Marsha, Pastor," she said. "She's a woman of God. Don't you worry. We're on your side. And the Lord is on your side, too. All this will blow over soon enough."

"That's right," Harvey added. He wrapped an arm around his wife's shoulders and squeezed.

The man in the middle of the church stood up slowly. He waited to be called on, no doubt so everyone would hear his name. The smirk on his face as much as told Daniel so.

"Yes, Clifford?" Daniel said.

Clifford Goins jumped right in.

"I got my haircut yesterdee, and the barber there—one of *your* people—was all excited about being *on call* that night. Wantin' to drive drunks around town and doin' it on behalf of this church. Now, I don't mind sayin', I don't think it's fittin'. Not a'tall."

The pain on Nikolas's face broke Daniel's heart. Innocent eyes glassed over with the hurt of false accusation. But something about the Grecian's sorrowful expression reminded Daniel of an important truth: Their Savior had been falsely accused, too.

Clifford sat back down. Unlike Agnes, he wore an expression of satisfaction.

"We are providing a service for people to help keep them safe," Daniel said. "And we are using that as an opportunity to witness to them." His tone was not reserved. "Nikolas Kostas is a faithful man of God who was excited for the chance to tell someone about Jesus."

Nikolas gave Daniel a grateful smile.

"Well, I didn't want to say it," Agnes spoke up from her seat, "but I do wonder if some of these rumors were brought on because of your association to that establishment. Service or not."

Harold Higgins, a tall, lanky man with a thin, straight mouth that stretched the width of his face, rose to his feet. "Pastor, I've heard about this taxi service. And as a member of the deacon board, I do have concerns. I would have rather spoken to you about it in private, but since you opened the floor, I'll speak my piece."

Daniel braced himself.

"You should have cleared it with all the deacons first before you used the church's name in such a way," Harold said. As he spoke, he sounded more hurt than angry. He finished and sat, and Daniel's jaw dropped an inch.

Daniel scanned the congregation for his comrades. Along with Harvey and Nikolas, Stewart and Homer were there, too. No doubt Alex was at work, and Greg was probably at home grading papers. But four fellow members of New Wine Transportation Company were at the ready to defend him. He felt it. Saw it in their eyes. And yet, Harold was right.

"Thank you for sharing how you feel, Harold," Daniel said. "While some of our deacons were aware of this project, I suppose it would have been best to consult with all of you. I apologize that it wasn't handled that way."

Harold's glance fell to the floor. "Well, it's okay, Pastor," he said, humbly. "I'm not sayin' you oughta stop. But maybe we can talk about it at the next board meeting."

"Absolutely," Daniel said.

He went back to the lectern and waited. No one else spoke up, but he gave them a chance until the silence became just as awkward as the conversation had been. He looked down at his study notes on the temptation of Jesus, but he didn't know where to start. The familiar verses on the page seemed like another language. He cleared his throat.

Clifford rose from his seat and left the sanctuary, and Daniel had to take a moment to gather his thoughts again.

"In the book of Matthew . . . "

He coughed and took a sip of water from the paper cup on the corner of the lectern.

"After Jesus was baptized . . . " he began again.

Daniel took out his handkerchief and wiped at the perspiration under his eyes, then opened his Bible. He squeezed his eyes shut tightly and took a deep breath. When he opened his eyes again, his heart pounding, he looked for the choir director. Like most of the congregation, Brenda sat in the same spot on the same pew every service. And seeing her there was an instant comfort. He had an escape.

With a wave of his hand, Daniel summoned the faithful musician to the front. She complied without hesitation, looking over her shoulder for the piano player, who also took the cue. Daniel whispered in her ear before taking his seat on the front pew of the far-right side.

For the next twenty minutes, they sang through one hymn after another, until the song leader's voice became hoarse. She looked at Daniel for permission to stop, and he nodded, then looked to Harvey.

"Can you dismiss us in prayer, please, Harvey?"

Daniel bowed his head to pray, but Harvey didn't say anything. He looked back. Maybe Harvey hadn't heard him. Daniel gave a nod in his direction and repeated the request. Still, no prayer. After another awkward moment, Harvey released his grip on the pew in front of him and stepped out into the aisle. He walked toward Daniel and beckoned other men to join him. Several men of the congregation gathered around their pastor as Harvey, with his large hand resting on Daniel's shoulder, began to pray aloud.

For the first few words of the prayer, Daniel's shoulders were tensed close to his ears. He was *their* shepherd. They relied on *him* to lead. And he had failed. But Harvey's petition soon began to soothe Daniel's weary heart. Surely, this powerful petition to the Almighty meant that Good would win, that Curtis's lies would be stopped, and that the whole church would rally around New Wine Transportation Company as the holy venture Daniel believed it to be, for however long the Lord had planned.

When the prayer was finished and people started heading for the door, Daniel thanked Harvey.

"I just want to do what the Lord wants me to do, Harvey," Daniel said.

"Then don't apologize for it." Harvey leaned in close and spoke quietly. "It was good for you to apologize to Harold for not consulting the board. I should have considered that, too. But don't apologize for carrying out the Lord's work. Even if nobody understands what you're doing."

Daniel looked up and locked eyes with his wise friend, wondering if he could see the real problem that weighed him down.

"Don't apologize, even if you don't understand the assignment yourself, Pastor," Harvey said gently. He placed his heavy hand on Daniel's shoulder again. "Nobody ever said you had to have all the answers. It's okay."

Harvey *did* understand. If anyone other than Marsha could see beneath all the complex layers of Daniel's role as pastor and understand that he struggled with the same doubts and fears as other believers—that his calling didn't make him invincible to earthly troubles—it was Harvey.

* * *

When Daniel came home from church, Marsha met him at the door and buried her face in his shoulder. Her normal Wednesday evening skirt and blouse were replaced with jeans and a flannel button-up. Only traces of makeup remained on her face, and the oversized shirt was covered in flour.

Daniel wrapped his arms around his wife, trying to absorb her sorrow in the embrace. He breathed in her familiar smell and the scent of cake in the oven. Baking was her stress-relief.

Marsha looked up, asking questions without words, speaking the silent language of long-time married people.

"It went okay," he told her. "Not great, but okay."

"But it's going to be okay, isn't it?" she asked.

He answered with a slight but confident smile that told her, "Eventually."

Tears welled in her eyes and threatened to spill out. "Mama called while you were at church," she said, sniffling. "She's heard."

Daniel dropped his head. "I'm so sorry, honey."

"My own mother! And I spent thirty minutes convincing her that it's not true. She kept saying, '*Are you sure* there's not something else you need to tell me?'"

"Oh, Marsha . . . " He held her and kissed the top of her head.

"Apparently, she got a phone call from Sherrill Baker—*bless her heart*—who said she was *worried* about me and wanted to know if she should *pray* for me." Marsha reached into her pocket for a tissue and dabbed at her nose.

There was nothing else to be said about the town's premier gossip. Bless her heart covered it all, for there was no malice. Sherrill was as generous as the day was long and as friendly a person as one would ever hope to meet. But when it came to "relaying news," she simply couldn't help it.

Daniel squeezed his wife a little tighter, shielding her from the world with his arms.

"But let's not talk about it anymore tonight," she said. She looked up at him, worry mingled with affection in her eyes.

It suited him fine. They could talk about it later. Now, it was time to clear their minds and just be together.

For the rest of the night, Daniel sat on the couch with Marsha, eating cake, while the smart speaker played jazz radio from the kitchen and Chewy purred quietly between them. On his second slice, it struck him—he ate his troubles in the same way some people drank them away. But the Cheerwine cake from Colleen Hill's cookbook was his favorite, and his wife had made it just for him. Just for him. That's how she did most things. How could he ever have doubted?

Since Daniel's phone didn't ring, it meant the streak of New Wine Transportation Company was broken, and he was glad. He couldn't have stood to hear one more thing about Main Street Bar that night. And at least Homer didn't have to go out. He'd looked so tired after service. Maybe it was asking too much of someone his age, anyway.

## Chapter Fourteen

New Wine Transportation Company, Driver Log
Date: Thursday, March 14
Driver: Stewart Bruce
Passenger: Monica Vance

IT WAS STILL DAYLIGHT, AND the tomato sandwich Stewart had scarfed down for dinner, right after he got the call from Daniel, still lingered on his taste buds. He hadn't expected to be called at all. Certainly not this early.

The woman standing outside his car door wore a low-cut blouse and too much makeup. Her face was two inches from the window, which he'd only rolled down a quarter of the way. Her perfume filled the car as if she were already inside.

"Are you my driver?" she asked.

A lump formed in Stewart's throat. "Yes, ma'am. I'm Stewart Bruce. At . . . a-a-at your service." He looked straight ahead as he spoke, already seeing more than he should in his peripheral.

"Oh, good." She opened the door of the hatchback and slid into the seat behind him. "I'm Monica. Joe told me you'd be picking me up. Thank you ever so much for the ride." The femininity of her voice ranked several notches above average.

Stewart risked making eye contact by glancing in the rearview mirror. Monica smiled like it was the first day of summer vacation as she swung her head from side to side, surveying the backseat. Her voluminous curls swayed with the motion of her head, revealing gold hoop earrings the circumference of a quart jar.

The car sat parked on the street in front of Main Street Bar with the engine running, and Stewart suddenly forgot how to make it move. He stared at the gear selector between the two front seats. *Prindle. What on earth is prindle? Has that always been there?*

"I live just across the train tracks," Monica chimed. "In the apartments."

Her persona was something from another time—a strange mix of Scarlet O'Hara and Julia Roberts from Pretty Woman.

Stewart's senses came to him, and he interpreted the letters on the gear selector. PRNDL. The *D* stood for "Drive."

"Oh, okay. I'll have you home in less than ten minutes then." No need to ask for directions. There was only one such complex in Springville.

Stewart's senses went haywire again as he pulled forward from the parking space and felt her closing in on the back of his head.

"Oh, excuse me," she said. "I need the mirror."

She used his rearview mirror to apply candy apple red lipstick, and with her closeness came an even more overwhelming scent of vanilla perfume. Stewart shifted this way and that; then with only one hand on the wheel, he adjusted the dashboard camera, pointing it directly at his passenger.

"Excuse me for saying so, Miss, but . . . you don't seem . . . I mean to say, you don't seem . . . impaired." He cleared his throat hard, sending a cough out at the end.

"You don't want to drive me home, do you?" In the mirror, he saw her bottom lip turned inside out and her long, not-possibly-real lashes batting repeatedly over eyes like Bambi's.

"No, no. It's not that at all. I'm happy to do it." He looked both ways at the stop sign, then turned right. Measuring his breathing, he thought back to the Saturday before in the basement of his church. He'd agreed to help anyone who asked for a ride. Too many questions weren't part of the assignment.

"I just wanted to be extra careful, that's all," she offered. "Don't you think it's good to be careful?"

"Oh, of course."

With hands gripping the wheel at ten and two, he drove the familiar roads toward the river and the old trainyard, going just below the speed limit.

"When I heard about your wonderful service—a ministry, I guess you'd call it—I thought it was the sweetest thing. I almost couldn't believe it when Joe told me. And I decided it was a good idea. Even after only one glass of wine, you just can't be too careful."

He nodded at her in the mirror. Definitely not the kind of passenger he expected, but a job was a job, and she was right. It was best to be careful. As an accountant, Stewart always double-checked his figures, made sure every *t* was crossed and *i* was dotted. He couldn't argue with her reasoning. He was as responsible as the day was long and had to appreciate that in this strange woman—if it really was her reasoning.

Stewart pulled into the apartments—two single-level buildings of five units, side-by-side. She didn't offer her apartment number, so he parked in between the buildings. Maybe she'd had second thoughts about a strange man knowing where she lived.

Stewart put the car in park. Monica opened the door just enough to let the March breeze slip in and stir around. The air played with the tiny tuft of hair that grew down into a point on the back of Stewart's neck.

Monica paused. "Silly me." Her palm smacked against her forehead. "I forgot that I'm supposed to go sit with my aunt Hilda tonight. She's been sick, and me and my sister and cousins take turns staying over there. Oh, mercy, she's plumb out in the country, and my car's back at the bar."

Stewart's eyebrows went high on his forehead. Maybe she'd had too much to drink after all. He tamed his face before she saw it in the mirror, not to risk her pouting again.

"Okay, that's no problem. No problem at all." He rechecked the angle of the dashboard camera. "Do you . . . do you want me to drive you over there?"

"You'd really do that for me? Oh, I can't believe how kind you are."

In response, he put the car in reverse and headed toward the driveway of the apartment buildings.

"Take a left outta here," Monica said.

"Yes, ma'am."

Monica sighed, starting two octaves higher than her speaking voice and sliding down to a normal tone. "You have such nice manners, Stewart," she said on the tail of the sigh, then giggled. "And so kind. I bet your wife really appreciates that about you."

"Wife? Oh, I'm-m-m, not m-m-married."

"Oh, I just assumed. A kind, nice-looking man like you."

Stewart's face suddenly felt like the aftermath of a five-day beach vacation and no sunscreen.

"But I'm not married either," she continued. "Came close about half a dozen times, but it never worked out. All the men I've ever dated were bums, two-timers, or both. Just can't seem to find Mr. Right, you know? Someone with a decent job and their own car, who doesn't do drugs and doesn't cheat. Someone who doesn't live with his mama."

The muscles in Stewart's shoulders tightened. He could have ignored it, but his meek nature was overtaken.

"I . . . I live with my mother," he said flatly.

Half of an embarrassed gasp escaped Monica's lips. "Oh. Well, I didn't mean . . . You probably live there to help her out, don't you?"

"She doesn't *need* me there, but yes, I help out plenty."

The sky had turned dark sometime between the time Stewart pulled up to Main Street Bar and then. The clouds concealed the moon, and there were no streetlamps along the way. Just Stewart and his passenger on an open country road.

"Oh, I'm so sorry," Monica said. "I didn't mean it like that. It's nice that you live with your mama. Really. I was just talkin' 'bout freeloaders, you know? Ones who take advantage."

Stewart cleared his throat. "Yes, I know. And I know the type."

Monica kept quiet for the rest of the drive, except to give directions to Aunt Hilda's house. Soon, Stewart steered the coupe onto the gravel drive of a tiny farmhouse. There were no other cars in the driveway, and no light came from the inside the house.

"Oh, no," she whispered. "What is today?"

"It's Thursday."

"You're gonna plumb hate me."

"Is there something the matter?"

"Thursday's my cousin Janice's turn to sit with Aunt Hilda. It's my turn tomorrow night."

Stewart swallowed hard. Something wasn't right. Monica hadn't even brought an overnight bag.

"Would you like for me to take you back to the apartments, Miss Vance?"

She hinted at yes with a sheepish, "Please, call me Monica."

Once again, the car went into reverse. With no need for directions, the car was quiet all the way back to Little Mill Apartments. When he returned to the same parking spot he'd used earlier, Monica reached her hand, clutching a crinkled bill, to the front seat over Stewart's shoulder. He reached up to take it, smiling at her in the mirror. As she slipped the bill into his open hand, she squeezed it gently and let hers linger. Stewart's ears grew hot.

Monica leaned back in the seat again but didn't open the door. "Don't you ever get lonely, Stewart?"

His head dropped, and he took a deep breath of courage. "Sometimes," he said softly. "But I'm never really alone. It may not be the kind of companionship you mean, but I take comfort in knowing that God is with me. And He's enough. If it's His will, He'll send the right woman—in His time."

"You're a remarkable man, Stewart Bruce."

Monica's voice was somehow different. He'd been called a lot of things, but never remarkable.

She sighed and continued. "I've never heard anybody talk about God like that. About not being alone. And to think, I never woulda heard it if it hadn't been for that glass of white wine." She smiled, and her brunette curls bounced again as she shook her head.

"The Lord works in mysterious ways, I suppose."

"I suppose He does."

All the way home, Stewart thought about his strange encounter, and before he went inside the house to watch game shows with his mother until bedtime, he took a little notebook and a pen from the glove compartment.

*Log Notes: Was that what I signed up for? I know the Lord has a plan, but tonight was unexpected, to say the least. Passenger wasn't intoxicated. Just seemed like she needed a friend. I hope God will send her what she needs. I'll pray for her tonight. Very unexpected.*

*Ten dollars collected for the camera fund.*

# Chapter Fifteen

BISCUITS AND GRAVY. THAT'S WHAT Daniel needed—a big plate of fluffy biscuits and peppery sausage gravy. After staying in seclusion with Marsha the day before, hiding from the whisperers in Springville, he was ready. He waited for the early morning crowd to clear, then headed to the diner for the Friday special.

Daniel spotted his favorite booth in the back corner, but he was stopped before he could sit down.

"Speedy, I didn't think you'd be back to work yet," Daniel said as the old man approached.

Speedy, whose wrinkled face seemed to have aged even more since the last time Daniel saw him, answered him with an unashamed embrace. No words. But Daniel's arms felt all that Speedy said. *I'm tired. I'm grieving. Thank you.*

Speedy released and wiped at his eyes. "Sit down, Preacher. Breakfast is on me today. You havin' the biscuits and gravy?"

"You know it."

Speedy went back to kitchen and, without being asked, a waitress came over with an empty cup and a pot of coffee. She smiled as she poured. Sheila was always kind. When was the last time he'd invited her to church? Too long ago, it seemed. He'd try again on the next visit.

Daniel grasped the cup with both hands and let its warmth soothe him. Within a minute, Speedy brought the food out and sat down.

"This looks great, Speedy. Thank you. I'm going to pray. Want to join me?"

Speedy bowed his head.

"Father, thank You for this food and thank You for another day of life. Thank You for the gift of friendship. Please continue to bless Speedy and his family in the days and weeks to come. Give them Your peace, Lord. Amen."

Daniel took the first bite. Nothing else like it. Better than filet mignon. He took a sip of coffee.

"So how *have* you been doing, Speedy? How are Rebecca's mom and dad?"

"We're breathing, Preacher. We're breathing." He flipped a hand towel onto his shoulder and leaned back in the booth. "Some days just seems like too much to handle, like we'll be crushed under the weight of it. But we keep going. And we will, with the good Lord's grace. It was the same way after my wife died. One day at a time."

Daniel nodded as he swallowed a bite. He'd had these conversations more times than he could count. The most predictable thing about life was the valley of the shadow of death.

"You know, the Psalms are a great comfort. Can I share some with you?"

"Thank you, but I'm okay. I got several of those verses right here." He tapped at his chest. "I don't want to talk about me, anyway. I want to know how *you're* doing."

Daniel searched Speedy's eyes. What did he mean? What did he know?

"I hear you've had a rough week, too," Speedy said.

Daniel took three bites in succession before he answered.

"So, you've heard about the owner of Main Street Bar and the rumors he's spreading about Marsha, huh?"

"I know it's all lies, of course. Most people do. But I'm worried for you. That's a lot to deal with—especially for a man whose career is partly built on reputation."

"Marsha wants me to talk to him, but I don't think I can. I might do something I'd regret, Speedy. I mean, I'm so angry. Not for myself, but for Marsha. She doesn't deserve this. But I know God can handle it, and I think it's best just to wait it out. He'll leave Springville soon, and we can forget about all of this."

"I'm sure sorry you're going through this, but I think you're right about not confrontin' him. Just let the Lord deal with it."

"The problem is this ministry. This . . . this service. No. This stupid idea I came up with and got my men involved in." His chest tightened. Was it really stupid? How had the doubt crept back in so quickly? He waited for reassurance from his friend that he hadn't made a mistake. But Speedy said nothing.

"I thought it would be once a week, at most," Daniel said. "But we've already had four calls. Four! In five days! I felt like we had an opportunity to witness. Point people to Jesus. But my men can't keep this up, and I want to distance my church as far as possible from Adam Curtis's bar *and* his lies."

Speedy leaned close. He opened his mouth as if to speak, then closed it again.

"I'm sorry, Speedy. I shouldn't be burdening you with this. You have much bigger problems."

"Pastor Whitefield—"

"I need to be a better counselor to you and not talk about . . . "

"Preacher—"

" . . . all this stuff that I've got going on. Please forget—"

"Daniel!"

Daniel stopped talking and sat a little straighter.

"Listen," Speedy said. "When you and I spoke last week about what to do about that bar, I saw a spark of something workin' in you. Then when I heard about what you were doing, this New Wine Transportation Company, it felt right to me."

"But I didn't know it would turn out like—"

"Daniel, I want you to keep doing what you're doing. Please. For me. Not because of Rebecca. But because there's some soul who needs to hear what the men of Springville Community Christian Church have to say. It's not stupid. It is a mission field. And, well . . . if God called you to it, you can't walk away from it."

Daniel let out a long, deep sigh. Speedy was right, of course. He'd have to keep walking this road, though he had no clue where it would end.

Speedy quickly changed the subject, but still, Daniel couldn't finish the biscuits and gravy. He sipped his coffee, letting it console him at least a little. The rest of his time in the diner was easier, as Speedy stepped further and further back from harsh truths that needed to be heard and offered Daniel something else that he needed—just his company.

\* \* \*

"We have the same habits, don't we, friend?" Reverend Reggie Carson called to Daniel from across the small parking lot of the diner. Daniel met him halfway.

"Daniel, I hate to hear that man is causing trouble for you," Reggie said as he shook his hand.

Yep, the whole town knew.

"Just remember—'no weapon formed against [you] will prosper.'[10] He can throw out lies like poison darts all around. They can't pierce you. They can't break you." A familiar electricity came from Reggie's hand resting heavily on Daniel's shoulder.

"Thank you, Reggie. You're right. It'll be okay."

Reggie gave him a knowing smile.

"I'll be praying for you tonight," Reggie said.

"Tonight?"

"Aren't you, uh . . . on call? It's your night, isn't it?"

"Oh, yeah. I guess it is. We'll see what happens, I guess. Thanks, Reggie."

How good it was to know that his spiritual mentor was back in his corner. If nothing else, their relationship had gotten stronger. There really was good in everything.

\* \* \*

New Wine Transportation Company, Driver Log
Date: Friday, March 15
Driver: Daniel Whitefield
Passenger: Richard Gambill

"What's the passengers name, Joe?" Daniel said into the phone.

"He didn't give it. But he's waiting in here at the bar. Want me to bring 'im out to ya, Preacher?"

---

10   Isaiah 54:17

"Is he that bad off?"

"I'll let you judge for yourself when you get here."

Out of the four other fares they'd taken so far, only one of them had been drunk. Funny how it had worked out that way. They'd transported a scared girl, a lying piece of work who took advantage of the service, and a lonely heart in search of a listening ear. Daniel felt a strange sense of satisfaction that he'd be getting to fulfill their original intention. Though it didn't seem right. He couldn't *want* someone to be too drunk to drive.

Within a few minutes, he was there. On either side of the door, several members of the League of Springville Churches mingled. Daniel recognized some of them as members of Reggie's church. Some held foam cups, and a large Thermos sat on the ground. They appeared to be on a coffee break.

Daniel waited, watching the front door, but Joe didn't come out. A couple minutes passed, still no one except the coalition. He drummed his fingers on the steering wheel and watched the limbs of a tree down the street bend in the March breeze beneath the light of a streetlamp. He checked his watch. 10:32. He'd give it three more minutes; then he'd have to go in.

At 10:35 p.m., Daniel got out of the car and walked up the sidewalk toward the building. A young lady wearing green earmuffs and a long chain necklace with a cross pendant as tall as a coffee mug took a step forward and smiled at him. "There's nothing good in there for you, friend," she said.

He started to answer, but a man on the other side of the walkway spoke up. "Josie, he's a preacher. This is Daniel Whitefield."

The girl with the green earmuffs looked embarrassed, then confused.

"Oh . . . well then . . . there's *really* nothing good in there for you," she said.

"It's okay," Daniel said. "I'm just here to—" He reached for the door as he spoke, but it opened first, and Daniel's brother-in-law stumbled out.

He reached to steady him. *This can't be happening,* Daniel thought.

"I told Joe not to call you," Richard said. "I'm fine. This isn't any of your business."

"Come on. Get in the car," Daniel ordered. He nodded a farewell to Josie and her friends as he turned.

Richard had righted himself and seemed to be making it down the sidewalk fine on his own.

"I told you, Daniel. I don't need you. My car is right down the street. I live two miles away. I'm fine."

They reached the street. "We'll help you get your car later," Daniel said. "Just let me take you home."

Richard slipped into the front seat of Daniel's car without any more argument. There was no need to turn on the camera that Stewart had brought him that morning.

Daniel was reeling. Maybe this was the whole assignment, just making sure Marsha's brother was safe. Could all of it be for this one encounter? He'd never have known about it otherwise. If the Good Shepherd left the ninety-nine to find one, maybe all Daniel's troubles were just so he could give Richard a ride home.

Richard's face was full of shame. He didn't seem *that* drunk, but enough. A member of the town council and chamber of commerce, drunk in public. It was disgraceful, even for Richard.

"Don't take me home, Daniel. I need you to take me to Springville Inn." Richard cleared his throat and rubbed at his temples.

"Why there?"

"Diane and I had a fight."

So, that's what the bender was about. *Do they fight a lot?* Daniel wondered. He and Richard had always been buddies, but not the kind who talked about problems—marital or otherwise.

"Hey, you know. These things happen."

"*Do they?* They don't seem to happen to you and Marsha. You're the perfect couple with the perfect life." His words slurred.

Daniel kept quiet as he headed in the direction of the hotel, praying for the right words. The line between brother-in-law and counselor was hard to cross. As they approached the destination, Daniel finally spoke.

"Would it help you to know that I slept on the couch Tuesday night? That doesn't sound so perfect, does it?"

Richard didn't hide his surprise and maybe a tinge of satisfaction.

Daniel parked the car two spaces from the front door and turned toward Richard.

"Look, we have problems, too. We're not perfect. But things work for us because we have Jesus. Both of us committed to putting Him first in our marriage. Sometimes, we miss the mark. But without Him, I'm not sure we'd stand a chance."

Richard's head fell back against the headrest of the seat, and he stared upward. "I don't want Marsha to know," he said. "About the fight . . . or about the ride."

It was a tough request. Daniel shared virtually everything with his wife. But he understood.

"Okay, Richard. I won't say anything."

"And especially not to Mother." Richard pointed a finger at him.

Daniel chuckled. "I wouldn't dream of telling Jackie," he said. "Nobody deserves that kind of punishment." Richard managed a grin. "Just promise me you'll think about what I said. There really is a better way."

"Yeah, well, maybe one day, I'll try it your way."

"That's good, buddy. But it's not just about having a good marriage. It's about your soul. None of us are promised another day."

Richard locked eyes with him. It seemed that something had clicked. The stupor lifted, and his eyes were clear with understanding. He nodded and shook Daniel's hand.

"Thanks for the ride, brother."

As Richard stepped from the car, Daniel's phone rang. It was Reggie's number.

"Daniel, I debated whether or not to call you," Reggie said.

*Not more bad news. I've had enough excitement for one night.*

"But I thought that, as a father, I would want someone to let me know."

"As a father? What are you talking about?"

"I just got down here to Main Street Bar. I'm, uh, takin' the late shift with the prayer vigil, and . . . well, I don't know any other way to say this. I just saw Claire go inside."

Daniel's jaw tightened, and a heaviness settled in his chest.

"*What?* I just came from there. What on earth would she be doing *there*? She's supposed to be at school. Are you sure it was her?"

"I'm sure, Daniel. I'm not trying to cause trouble; I just—"

"She's only twenty. I don't understand."

Confusion turned to anger. It couldn't be. Not his little girl. She was a good girl.

Daniel thanked Reggie for calling and disconnected the call as he put the car into reverse; then he sped away from the parking lot of Springville Inn on a mission.

## Chapter Sixteen

THE SOUND OF "AMAZING GRACE" filled Daniel's ears as he passed the group outside Main Street Bar. More from Reggie's church had joined the others, and they stood on either side of the walk like before, huddled together against the cold. He didn't make eye contact with any of them, but he silently blessed them for their anthem. What had seemed so unnecessary before, now seemed just for him.

Daniel pushed open the door of the bar like it was the swinging door of a Wild West saloon and he was the new sheriff in town. He stopped three feet inside and scanned. The bar was rather plain, not the made-over place Curtis had bragged about at The Soda Shop. The crowd was much sparser than he'd expected for a Friday night, too.

He spun around, searching for Claire. In his mind's eye, the place was as it used to be. A handful of people sat at the bar that once-upon-a-time had been a cosmetics counter. More empty tables than not were placed where racks of clothing once stood. There was only one television mounted to the back wall, the same wall that once housed large rows of rectangular signs advertising the different brands of shoes available. Maybe downstairs was more impressive.

"Dad, I can explain."

Daniel turned at the sound of his daughter's voice as she came from the ladies' restroom. A mix of emotions flooded his heart.

"I know you can, honey. And you can do it at home. Let's go." He took her by the elbow and started for the door, but she pulled away.

"No, I can't leave. It's my friend. She's here, and I need to help her." She held on to Daniel's forearm. "I was coming home to surprise you tonight, Daddy, but Emma called me while I was on the road. She asked me to come get her."

"You should have called me, Claire."

"Daddy, there wasn't time. She needed me."

He examined her innocent, pleading eyes. So much like her mother. Claire would do anything to help a friend.

"Where is she? What's the matter? Is she hurt?"

"She's in the bathroom. Just sick. I don't even know why they let her in here, but she's had too much to drink. I'm going to take her home."

Maybe Claire was a little like him, too.

Daniel looked around, suddenly aware that people were watching them. It didn't matter. He'd had no choice but to come in after his underage daughter. And it seemed she had no choice either.

"Wait, how old is Emma?" he asked.

"Eighteen, Daddy. She heard they didn't ask for ID here. It's been all over social media how easy it is to get in. And most kids just want to see if it's true, just for kicks. She came with some other friends, and they all drank; but when she got sick, they got scared of getting busted and left her here."

"Okay, then, take care of your friend," he said. "Try to get her out of here as soon as possible. Want me to stay and ride with you?"

"No, it's fine. She's already so embarrassed, Daddy. She'd die if you saw her now. I think she's learned a lesson."

He took her hands in his. "Be safe, baby girl. I'll see you at home."

He leaned to hug her but froze, then straightened slowly at the sound of a familiar voice.

"Well, well, Daniel Whitefield. What are you doing here?"

Daniel turned to see Curtis leaning against the bar with a toothpick hanging from the corner of his Cheshire cat grin. Curtis sauntered a few steps closer.

"None of your business, Curtis," Daniel said. The time for being nice was over. All his previous attempts had been like casting pearls before swine.

Curtis ignored him and came close enough for his cologne to assault Daniel's nose. Daniel stepped in front of Claire and reached behind him to hold her there.

"Say, you're not stepping out on Mrs. Whitefield, now, are you? With this young thing?"

His sleazy laugh was mocking, but Daniel wasn't going to be baited. He couldn't fall into Curtis's trap. *Be angry, and do not sin,*[11] he whispered to himself.

"This is my daughter, Curtis. And like I've already said, what I'm doing here is none of your business, and neither is she. So back off."

Curtis circled them like a hungry shark. Daniel pivoted to keep himself between Claire and Curtis.

Curtis took the toothpick from his mouth and pointed it. "Say now. She sure is a hot, little number." He laughed. "I'm not certain, but I think she might be even sexier than her mother."

With one quick lunge, Daniel's fist met Curtis's face; then Curtis hit the floor with a thud.

---

11  Ephesians 4:26a

Claire let out a scream, and Joe ran from behind the bar and squatted down beside Curtis. What a relief it was to hear Curtis let out the slightest groan as Joe yelled his name.

Daniel turned back to his daughter. "It'll be okay, Claire. Go get Emma and get her out of here. I want you *both* out of here now."

"But, Daddy—"

"Everything will be okay, sweetie. Tell mom I'm fine. *Everything will be fine.* Just go home."

Claire was shaking, but she obeyed.

A meager crowd began to gather at the front of the room. Daniel's heart raced. His instinct said to get out fast and not look back. But he couldn't. He had to face responsibility for what he'd done. But what would it look like? An apology? He *wasn't* sorry.

A trickle of blood ran from Curtis's purple lip, as he lifted his head off the floor. Daniel walked behind the bar and found a stack of folded rags. He took the top one from the stack and took it to Joe, who had his phone pressed against his ear and was giving the address of the bar.

Daniel walked outside to wait. For what exactly, he didn't know.

The March air shocked his senses. The singing had stopped, but a smaller group prayed quietly nearby. He stepped close to the group but didn't join in. Not even close enough to hear their words, but the action was comforting, nonetheless. The spirit of it, the Spirit in it— it kept him sane, from running for the car to hide in shame or back in to punch Curtis again. He checked his phone to see a text message from Marsha.

*Praying for you. I'll wait up.*

He put the phone back in his pocket. Suddenly, the trees and sidewalk in front of the bar were illuminated in blue. There was no siren, but the lights were enough. The group stopped praying. Should he call Marsha now and tell her why he'd be late or wait and let her hear it from Claire?

Some of the patrons of the bar filed outside and began mingling with the prayer group, whispering to one another and pointing at Daniel. More patrons came outside. Some made fast getaways upon seeing the deputy's car.

The officer who emerged from the patrol car was no stranger. Jason Green was engaged to Harvey and Colleen's daughter, Melody, and Daniel was all set to perform the ceremony in June. Should he be relieved or upset that it was him? Would they still want a preacher with a rap sheet?

"Pastor Whitefield, are you okay?" Deputy Green asked.

"I'm okay, son."

The tall, handsome deputy gently took Daniel by the elbow, and in a sympathetic voice he said, "I think you better come back inside and tell me what happened."

When all was said and done, Jason Green had no choice but to place Daniel under arrest. The crease in the deputy's brow and the downward turn of his mouth reminded Daniel of himself when he'd had to punish Claire when she was little. His expression said, *This hurts me more than it hurts you.* And it multiplied Daniel's shame.

No handcuffs were required—a small blessing. The ride to the county jail in the back of the car was traumatic enough with free hands.

## Chapter Seventeen

EARLY IN HIS MINISTRY, DANIEL had delivered an entire eulogy addressing the deceased by the wrong name. When Claire was a baby, he left her alone for just a moment, and she rolled off the bed, leaving a pop-knot on her forehead. During the homecoming game his senior year of high school against their biggest rival, he drew a penalty that cost them the game. On any given day, these memories floated around in the back of his brain, and they occasionally popped to the front long enough to make his shoulders slump. But this topped them all. Punching Adam Curtis was like all three mess-ups combined, times ten. Those had been mistakes, not matters of character. This one could follow him for the rest of his life, maybe even cost him the pulpit. And there was nothing he could do now. That would be up to the deacon board.

He looked from face to face. All six of the men around the table of the Sunday school room—this time a more accommodating space—waited for him to speak, all with the same anxious and slightly uneasy expression. Harvey, Nikolas, Greg, Stewart, and Alex all leaned in with anticipation. All except Homer, who lounged back in the folding metal chair, looking more sleepy than concerned, with his hand tucked in the front pocket of his overalls. What would each of them think? How would they respond? They couldn't possibly understand his position.

"Men, thank you once again for meeting me on a Saturday morning." Daniel started out like conducting a business meeting but soon slid into the familiar cadence of conversing with friends. "A week ago, we had lofty ideals, an ambition to do something for God." A couple of the men bobbed their heads in a slow, rhythmic nod of remembrance.

"You took on my challenge for a ministry that had no precedent," Daniel said. "But . . . well, things haven't turned out like I'd hoped." He looked away from the men and addressed the wall. "Funny to think it's only been a week. Feels like at least a month." Defeat wrapped him up in sadness.

Nikolas spoke up. "'A man's heart plans his way, But the LORD directs his steps.'[12] Things don't have to turn out like you had hoped for it to still be God's will." He paused. "Oh, forgive me, Pastor. I—"

"No, you're right, Nikolas. I need reminding of Scripture just as much as anybody else." He held up a reassuring hand. "He *does* direct our steps, but sometimes, we veer off course." Daniel scanned the faces again and took a deep breath. "I know you've all heard what happened last night at Main Street Bar, and I want you to know that I am very sorry about it. I wasn't at first. I admit it. I felt justified. But after some soul-searching, I realize there is no excuse for my actions. I should have been able to keep my cool. I did not represent this church well, and I did not represent Jesus well."

With an uncharacteristic brashness, Harvey slapped the tabletop. "Daniel, let me tell you right now, I like to think I'm a mild-mannered guy. Most say a big teddy bear. But if anyone had said about Melody what that man said about Claire, he'd be lucky to leave with only a fat lip." The two other fathers nodded in agreement.

---

12    Proverbs 16:9

"I thank you for that, Harvey," Daniel said. "Still, I know I have to face the consequences. And while spending a couple hours at county jail last night, I decided that it is probably best to discontinue our project. They're not going to want to have anything to do with us, anyway. Not after what I did. I think we can formally disband New Wine Transportation Company."

The room was quiet, save for the nearly silent tapping of Stewart's fingers on the table.

Greg was the first to speak again. "Pastor, I know things haven't turned out like you hoped, but . . . well, I wouldn't say this week has been a total loss. My passenger really did need a ride, and he may not have gotten home safely without me. He has a wife and two kids, too. I guess I just mean that we can't know whether or not it saved his life, but it *is* possible. And either way, I think it helped . . . somehow."

With his arm bent and fingers pointed upward, Stewart raised his hand to eye level. Daniel smiled and nodded *yes*.

"I guess I did talk about the Lord, at least a little bit, with the lady I drove home," Stewart said. "Nice lady. Very lonely. She seemed interested in what I had to say, so . . . so, maybe it will make her think. Maybe. She might even come to church sometime."

"Oh, yes, definitely," Nikolas said. His enthusiasm balanced Stewart's meekness. "And in my car, that foul man heard songs about Jesus on the radio. Certainly, God can use that if He wants to. We were obedient; the rest is up to the Almighty."

Whatever they had accomplished, at least Daniel could rest assured he'd picked the right men for the task. And they had done some good during their short-lived effort.

"I know that Harvey and Colleen invited a young lady to church. So, there's that, too," Daniel said. Harvey nodded, his eyebrows raised in affirmation. "And the person I drove last night, well, I believe the Lord will reach him soon. So, you're right. God did work through this mission."

All the men had contented smiles, except for two of them.

"Alex, is something wrong?" Daniel said.

Alex shrugged his shoulders and shoved his hands into the pockets of his faded denim jacket. "Oh, no, Pastor. I'm fine. It's just that, I didn't get a chance to go out. I was hoping I'd get a call tonight. I had a feeling I might . . . well, it sounds silly."

"No, what is it?" Harvey said.

"I just had a feeling I might be able to help someone."

Daniel sighed. It was too bad Alex had to miss his chance to help on account of him. But surely, Joe wouldn't call the man who had punched his boss, not even if someone really needed a ride.

"I'm sorry, Alex," Daniel said. "I know you were looking forward—"

"We're not done, Pastor," Homer interrupted. He sat up straight, took off his hat, and looked around the table at each of them. "I can't tell you why or when we *will be* finished or what it's all about. But my spirit says we ain't done. It's kind of like when your joints ache when it's going to rain, and you just know it." He looked back to Daniel. "Of course, *you're* the man of God."

Just like the week before, Daniel choked on his emotions. He studied the wise, old man for a moment; then he whispered a silent prayer for wisdom such as his.

"If there's any man of God here, Homer, I'm looking at him." Daniel took a deep breath and clasped his hands together. "I guess we'll just see if Joe calls. And if he does, I'll tell him we have the men for the job."

Alex brightened and nodded in agreement at Daniel. Homer gave the pastor a wink.

"Another good thing, a very good thing, that seems to have come out of our *association* with Main Street Bar," Daniel said, "is that we've learned about and have been able to report underage drinking there. All I know is that it's being investigated."

"My soon-to-be son-in-law took a statement from me and Colleen about the little girl we drove home," Harvey said. "She was only seventeen. She had no business being in that place."

"And I was able to tell him about Claire's friend who was there last night," Daniel said. The problem is, of course, it's all hearsay, and those young people are probably too afraid of getting into trouble to talk to the sheriff's department. But if they can prove it, there will definitely be repercussions for the bar."

"And what about you, Pastor? Do you know what the repercussions will be for you?" The question came from Nikolas, but they all must have been wondering the same thing.

"No. I don't know yet," Daniel said. "With the law, with the church—I don't know. I guess like with a lot of things, we'll just have to wait and see."

At Harvey's leading, all the men stood and, once again, made a prayer circle around their pastor. Several strong hands rested on his shoulders and the top of his head, and he was comforted under the weight of them. A holy presence filled the room as they presented Daniel's troubles to the only One who could help.

## Chapter Eighteen

"IF THE CHURCH FIRES ME, I think we should go on a cruise." Daniel said. He put his arm around Marsha's shoulders. "I'm thinking the Bahamas, or maybe Cancun. We haven't been able to take a break in years."

"Me, too?" Claire called from the kitchen.

"Of course, you, too!" Daniel called back. "You can be our tour guide."

"And how would we pay for this cruise if you have no job?" Marsha asked. She gave him a wink.

"We'll just dip into that huge savings account we have. No problem."

"Oh, well in that case, we should sail around the world, maybe spend a month off the coast of France," Marsha said. She chuckled, and the sound chipped away a tiny bit of the angst that gripped his heart.

"Nah, I don't think we want to leave Chewy for that long."

Daniel dealt with uncertainty in two ways—prayer and humor. And he'd already spent a great deal of time in prayer. God would work it out. There was no doubt. Still, he couldn't help wondering what was going to happen at the church. While he spent the Saturday evening at home with his family, the deacons were gathered in an emergency meeting.

"Oh, honey, I forgot to tell you," Marsha said. "Mary Jane Jenkins called earlier. She said Timothy has to have some kind of tests on Monday. I told her you would wait with her at the hospital, and I would watch the other four kids at her house."

Daniel nodded. "Sounds good."

Whether the church fired him or not, the congregation would still be their family, too.

Claire brought them a bowl of popcorn from the kitchen and plopped into the recliner with her own bowl. "Okay, let's start the movie, Daddy."

Seeing her in her jogging outfit with her long brown hair twisted up into a messy bun reminded him of the days when they spent most Saturday nights together. As long as he wasn't ministering somewhere, he was with them. And it was his favorite place to be.

As Daniel reached for the remote, his cell phone rang, and he froze. Family nights were becoming more and more rare. And he had so much on his mind. Maybe he could just ignore the call. Probably a telemarketer, anyway.

He hit play on the remote, and the ringing of the phone stopped as the intro music started up. Before the credits began, the phone rang again, and Daniel let out an exasperated sigh.

Claire grinned and shot him a look that said, *You know you're going to answer that.*

He smiled back as he picked up the phone. She'd been raised this way, where he was always on call and never clocked out. She understood.

He looked at the number and blinked hard. It couldn't be. He'd been sure it wouldn't happen. Not when just the night before, he'd . . .

"Hello?" Daniel answered. It was safe to interrupt family night for just a moment. The call wasn't really for him, anyway. He'd be taking a message for Alex Martinez.

\* \* \*

New Wine Transportation Company, Driver Log

Date: Saturday, March 16

Driver: Alex Martinez

Passenger: Two Men, Business Associates of Adam Curtis

Alex's Bible lay open on the front seat of his Mustang to the passage he'd read before leaving his house. *But those who wait on the LORD Shall renew their strength; They shall mount up with wings like eagles, They shall run and not be weary, They shall walk and not faint.*[13] After working two plumbing emergency calls on his day off, then helping a friend with a leaky faucet, he needed those words. Now he was ready for the next job God had for him.

He stood beside the red car—its polished hood gleaming in the light of the streetlamp—hands clasped in front of him, ready to greet his passengers. All he knew about them is that they were out-of-towners, businessmen who needed a ride. That's what Pastor Whitefield had told him because that's what Joe had told Pastor Whitefield.

Alex rocked from one sneakered foot to the other as he waited. He looked down at his clothes, wondering if he should have changed. Most drivers probably dressed much like he did, except for the limousine drivers in the movies, with their fancy suits and caps. He wore jeans and a dark red t-shirt covered by a denim jacket. It would

---

13   Isaiah 40:31

have to be okay. He'd rushed over there as to not keep them waiting, though now it seemed like there'd been no need to hurry.

Alex practiced his smile and, in his head, rehearsed a greeting. He turned to the driver side window, and his reflection looked back at him. A big smile was out of the question. It seemed fake. He tried again. One side turned up seemed to be the one. Friendly, but not too pushy.

Another few minutes passed. Alex thought about getting back inside the warm car to wait but wouldn't let himself. He wanted to greet the men properly and make a good impression. Even though they weren't from Springville, if they planned to stay for a while, he could invite them to church. And if he made a good impression, they might accept.

Finally, two men came out of the bar who were unmistakably not from Springville. One was short, and he wore a dark suit and had slicked back hair. The other was a large man, and he wore a dark leather jacket and dark glasses, though it was 8:00 p.m.

"Good evening," Alex called to them. "Chilly tonight, isn't it?"

The big man in the leather jacket motioned a greeting, but neither spoke. When they reached the car, the big man dove into the backseat, while the other approached.

"I'm Alex Martinez," Alex said to the man in the suit. "I'm from New Wine Transportation Company, an outreach ministry of Springville Community Christian Church." Alex extended a hand, but the man didn't take it. Alex chuckled at nothing and stuck his hand in his pocket.

"Where can I take you this evening, sir?"

"Hey, I'm gonna cut to the chase," the man in the suit said. "We just need a ride to the hotel. Okay? No chit chat. No small talk. And especially no preaching. Just a ride. Capisce?"

Alex's jaw tightened. He remembered Nikolas's turn, how rude the man had been. This wasn't supposed to be a taxi service. Not a real one. But he guessed service of any kind could be the Lord's work if He willed it, whether the people appreciated it or not.

"Yes, sir," Alex said. He nodded at the man and opened his door. He'd just to have to turn on his radio, like Nikolas had done.

"Man, the basement was crowded tonight." The large man had moved the shades to the top of his head. He shifted his weight in the seat.

Alex pulled away from the curb and headed for the stoplight as he turned on soft praise and worship music.

"Yeah, business is picking up," the man in the suit said. "Still not sure this tiny town's gonna be worth my time, though."

Alex bristled at the disgust in the man's voice. Springville was more than just a place to live. It was his home, and there was nowhere else like it.

"I didn't think you had a choice." The big man laughed.

Alex took his eyes off the road for a moment and looked in the rearview mirror to see the man in the suit glare at the other man.

"For sure, I wouldn't waste my time if it wasn't . . . well, if it wasn't in my best interest."

"You mean, if Curtis hadn't threatened to squeal."

"Hey, lower your voice."

Whatever they were talking about, the man in the suit didn't want Alex to hear it, which made him tune in even more to the conversation.

"He says you owe him some money, too. How much does he have you in for, Gorski?" the big man said.

"Shut up, Ace. I mean it."

Alex gripped the steering wheel and made himself keep his eyes fixed straight ahead.

The man in the suit lowered his voice even more, but its baritone carried to the front of the car. "First off, it's none of your business. Second, we can talk at that dump they call a hotel. But I ain't lettin' Curtis pin all his dirty dealings on me. He's the one who started that operation in the basement. I'm just an advisor. Gambling is my *spesh*-iality."

*Gambling.* Had he heard that right? He had definitely heard one of them say *dirty dealings.* They were up to no good, for sure, but was illegal gambling really going on at Main Street Bar? That kind of thing just didn't happen in Springville. At least, it didn't use to. They must have thought he was an idiot, to talk in front of him.

Alex mustered the courage to speak as he pulled into a parking space in front of the little hotel.

"Here we are, gentlemen. I hope you have a good evening. And God bless you both."

The man in the suit, the one called Gorski, didn't respond as he stepped out of the car.

"Thanks for the ride, fella," Leather Jacket said.

Alex cracked his window to let in some fresh air and heard Gorski say, "Hey, can you believe these chumps are doing it for free?"

Gorski strutted toward the hotel, but the big man ducked his head back into the car and tossed a bill into the front passenger seat. Alex turned and locked eyes with him for a moment.

"Good night," the man said. He smiled, then closed the door before Alex could speak.

Alex crooned his neck to watch him. The man looked from left to right, scanning like a crossing guard, as he traversed the parking lot to catch up to his associate. Only after his passengers had entered the hotel did Alex look at the money the man in the leather jacket had dropped onto the seat beside him—a hundred dollar bill. His skin tingled as a breeze came from the open window. A hundred dollars. But why had he done it? He picked up the bill and ran his fingers along the edges. Hadn't pastor said the ministry would pay for itself? Of course—the exact cost of the cameras had been tossed their way after six nights and only one small donation.

The chill turned into a warm sensation on his cheeks as Alex bowed his head there in the parking lot and thanked God. Tomorrow, he would be able to give the money to Pastor Whitefield.

*The camera.* He'd turned it on before the passengers had even entered the car. The entire backseat conversation had been recorded, if the sound picked up. Maybe he should take the memory card to the authorities and let them know something seemed shady. He could call his buddy Jason to see what he thought. It certainly couldn't hurt. The sheriff's department was already investigating the underage drinking claim. Maybe there was more to find out.

## Chapter Nineteen

EARLY SUNDAY MORNING, LONG BEFORE anyone would walk through the front doors of the church, Daniel sat in the small pastor's study behind the sanctuary, holding an envelope addressed to him. He'd come to adjust the thermostat, to study, and to pray that he wouldn't be fired and that Agnes Reynolds wouldn't take him to task in front of everyone, along with the normal things he prayed for each Sunday morning before the service. Now, there was a distraction.

He held the envelope by the corner and tapped the edge against the desk over and over to the rhythm of the second hand on the clock on the wall. His name was hand-written on the front. No address and no postmark. He had found it taped to the door of the church when he got there.

He leaned back in the cushy, leather chair—a gift from the congregation for his twentieth anniversary of the start of his ministry. He ran his hand back and forth on the cool armrest. Daniel's Bible lay open on the desk in front of him to the book of Job. He needed to brush up on his sermon, clear his mind to prepare to preach, though if the envelope contained a pink slip, there would be no need.

*No. They wouldn't do it that way. Surely not.*

He knew he could count on Harvey, but most of the deacons had been silent.

Maybe it was a complaint letter from Agnes. It wouldn't be the first he'd received from her.

He leaned forward again, took a big drink from the insulated mug of coffee he'd brought from home, then held the envelope with both hands, staring a hole through it.

"I just have to open it," he said. He took a deep breath. "God, this is in Your hands. Whatever happens, let it be Your will."

He carefully tore off the top of the envelope and took out a single piece of paper folded in half. He unfolded the letter and his eyes went straight to the signature scribbled at the bottom. In letters three times the size of the rest of the writing, it was signed *Curtis*.

Daniel braced himself to read the note. His heart pounded and his mouth went dry. He took another sip of coffee. Maybe he should wait until after the sermon to read it, so as to not cloud his mind. But he couldn't help it. The paper rattled in his hands as he read the simple message at the top.

*You've made a big mistake, Daniel.*

*Payback is coming. Trust me.*

Daniel dropped the paper on the desk and stood as if he'd heard a fire alarm. But he didn't run. He paced with quick steps in front of his desk with his head down. In the small space, with shelves of books on three walls, he walked in a circle as he prayed for the rage to subside.

Curtis's threat didn't scare Daniel; it made him angrier than he'd ever been in his life. It churned in his belly. It made him hope Curtis *would* try something, just to give him another excuse to hurt him. It was an anger that he knew crossed the line—the line that Scripture spoke of. *Be angry, and do not sin.*[14] He'd crossed it before when he punched Adam Curtis in the face. But how could he control it?

Daniel stopped pacing and flung open the door of his study. He scanned the sanctuary. Empty, as he expected. A good thing. He needed to be alone with God.

His palms were sweaty and his head throbbing as he dropped on his knees and laid his body on the alter. The rough, red carpet was comforting and familiar to his face.

"Only You can fix this," Daniel said.

No more words came, but he waited in the silence, willing the emotion that bordered hatred to leave his heart and mind. Then in a single word, he felt the answer. *Forgive.*

He'd known it all along. It was so simple. Unforgiveness was the root of the anger that plagued him. For all Daniel's remorse about punching Adam Curtis in the face, and his shame about being arrested, the flame of unforgiveness for the pain Curtis had caused grew daily within his heart. And the letter had stoked the fire.

If it were only him, he could have handled it. But Curtis had hurt Marsha with his lies. He'd hurt his congregation. He'd disrespected Claire. That's what made it so hard.

He sat up and wiped at his face, then looked at the giant cross on the wall. *Forgiveness.*

Daniel checked his watch. Sunday school would be starting in only thirty minutes. In an hour and a half, it would be time for the worship service—time to face his congregation and see if he could

---

14   Ephesians 4:26

read how they felt about him now. Or maybe they would tell him. Their pastor was a criminal.

*Why did it have to be today?* he thought. *Today is already hard enough.* He picked himself up off the floor and stood in front of the altar. His mind went to the words he said just before opening the letter. Of course. He'd prayed for God's will to be done. *God's will,* not his. Now, he had to have faith. The letter hadn't come as a surprise to God. And what someone meant for evil, God could use for good.

He shoved his hands in his pockets and looked at the floor. Maybe the letter was just what he needed to be pushed to this point—the point he realized he had no choice but to forgive Adam Curtis.

# Chapter Twenty

"YOUR SERMON WAS GREAT, HONEY, but I . . ."

"Go ahead. What is it?" Daniel asked.

"But I could tell you were distracted."

Marsha stood next to Daniel at the back of the sanctuary, whispering to him during the closing prayer.

"Don't let anything that anybody says get to you. It's going to be okay." She held his hand with locked fingers and gave it a firm squeeze. "We're in this together. And your congregation loves you. They'll support you." Her whispers tickled his ear.

Daniel squeezed her hand in response but kept quiet. She assumed it was only the arrest that bothered him. He'd have to tell her about the note later.

The prayer went on and on, as he expected. He'd asked the most long-winded person to lead it. That gave him more time to gather himself.

"Crowd was up today. I think we have some visitors," Marsha said.

At the sound of amen, people began filing out of the pews.

"Oh, good," Daniel said at a normal volume. "I didn't notice."

Marsha kept her whisper even though the prayer was over. "See, I knew you were distracted."

Parishioners began to pass by with the normal handshakes, smiles, and salutations. He read between the lines of each one, analyzing each brief encounter.

*Did she tense up when she took my hand?*

*He seemed fine, I think.*

*Did he avoid eye contact?*

Some made straight for the lobby without stopping to shake hands, but it wasn't unusual.

Marsha's voice as she greeted each passerby in her warm, genuine way soothed his heart and bolstered his confidence.

More handshakes, more smiles. Still no mention of the *incident.*

Then came Agnes. He tensed when he saw her. In her printed dress, black with giant white flowers and a lacy collar, she had the appearance of a harmless, old woman. But Daniel saw the armor underneath. Agnes was always ready to battle about something.

"Good morning, Agnes," he said. Cheerfulness was the goal. So far, so good.

"I have to say I'm surprised by you, Daniel," Agnes said as Daniel shook her hand. "Truly, very surprised."

"I know, Agnes, and I—"

"I didn't know you had it in you." She was stalwart.

"I understand, and there's no—"

"According to everything I've heard"—she pointed a finger in his face—"and by all accounts, it occurs to me that you did *exactly* what had to be done on Friday night."

Daniel's mouth dropped. He was speechless.

"I *respect* a man who defends his family." Her tone was that of a commanding officer saluting a subordinate. Without another word, she shook Marsha's hand and sidled to the lobby, the giant purse hanging from the crook of her arm rubbing against her hip as she went.

Marsha and Daniel looked at each other with wide eyes. Had that really just happened?

Daniel turned back to see that a stranger was next in line to greet him.

Big hair, big earrings, and a smile to match, the lady reached her hand out first, and Daniel shook it.

"It's nice to have you with us today," he said. "Thank you for coming. What's your name?"

"I'm Monica Vance," she said with a nod.

"Well, we're glad you're here, Monica. Do you know anyone in the congregation?"

"I see lots of familiar faces," she said. "But everybody's familiar in Springville, aren't they?"

"That's true."

"But see that man over there?" Monica pointed into the lobby at Stewart. He stood against the wall holding his mother's coat while she chatted with two other ladies.

"Oh, Stewart." Daniel smiled and nodded.

"He drove me home the other night," she said.

Of course, her name had seemed familiar. He'd read it in the driver log that Stewart turned in.

"There was just something so different about him," Monica said. Her voice was full of admiration, and she leaned in, talking to both Daniel and Marsha. "He was so kind and decent. Just . . . well, I can't even explain it. But I thought if men like that come to church, then maybe that's where I should go to meet one."

Monica giggled.

"Well, you can't get much better than Stewart Bruce," Marsha said. "Except for my husband, of course, and he's taken." She smiled at Monica, then offered her an arm. "Come on, let's get the two of you reacquainted," she said. The two linked arms and started toward the lobby.

Monica called back over her shoulder to Daniel.

"Don't worry. Your sermon was good. If this doesn't work out, I'll probably come back just for the preaching."

Daniel waved and gave her a grateful smile. What a morning it was turning out to be. Too many emotions in a ten-minute span left him trying to catch his breath.

The line had dwindled. Some people remained inside the sanctuary, huddled in little groups. Others had moved on to the lobby. *Visiting.* That's what it was called. Sunday after service was a good time to *visit* with one another. If only for a moment, it kept them connected, fueled by the concern and care of others until next week. He smiled as he spied on them from his post at the door of the sanctuary.

He greeted a few more as they left, then headed back toward the pulpit to gather his things. Half-way up the aisle, someone called out, "Pastor Whitefield?"

Daniel turned to see a young woman approaching. Two girls followed behind her. He knew their faces. For three months he'd noticed them, but they always ducked out before service was over.

"Good to see you," he said. "I don't believe we've actually met."

"I'm Jennifer Hupert," she said. "And these are my girls, Amy and Amber."

"Hi, there," Daniel said to the children.

The girls, one maybe twelve and the other around seven, offered timid smiles.

"I just wanted to say thank you," Jennifer said. She reached into her purse and brought out a little New Testament with an orange cover. "My husband came home the other night, and he had this in his shirt pocket. When I looked at it the next morning, I found this."

Jennifer opened the Bible and pointed to the church's name and address stamped inside the cover. She looked at Daniel with tears in her eyes.

"Me and the girls have been coming here, and then somebody from our church picks T.J. up from the bar on a Monday night and brings him home. What are the odds of that?"

Chills ran down Daniel's back like electric waves.

"I just wanted to let you know he's been reading it," she said. "I caught him a couple days ago, but I didn't let him know it. I've been tryin' for years . . . And he's drinkin' less the last couple days, too."

Words escaped him. Seeing the very hand of God at work had tied his tongue. Someone's daddy was drinking less. Someone's husband was reading the Bible.

When Daniel recovered, he prayed with them out loud—for T.J. and for them. Pouring forth, yet from an empty well, the words he found were not his own.

\* \* \*

Only a few cars remained in the church parking lot.

Daniel and Marsha walked hand-in-hand to the car. He felt revived as he told her what had happened inside the church, and the anger he'd felt in the study that morning was a distant memory.

"It's amazing, honey. To think that Greg would be the one to drive her husband home and that he gave him a Bible."

"Just mind-blowing," she said. "And what about our guest? I think she and Stewart might actually hit it off."

"I saw you playing matchmaker."

She flashed a mischievous grin at him as he opened her car door.

"Could there be any more surprises today?" he asked.

"Hey, Pastor Whitefield!" someone called from across the parking lot.

Daniel closed Marsha's door as Alex Martinez jogged toward him from where his Mustang was parked.

"Hey, Pastor! I don't want to hold you up, but—"

"Hey! How'd it go last night? I tried to find you earlier, but then I got busy."

"Oh, it was fine. Two guys. Um . . . *businessmen*. Just dropped them off at the hotel."

"Good, good. Thanks for going out. I'm still surprised that Joe called us."

"Yeah, well, it seemed like they just needed a taxi." He flashed a sheepish grin. "I think one of them may have been the same guy Nikolas drove."

"I see."

"Yeah."

Daniel sighed. The man that Nikolas drove was the ring leader of the rumor mill.

"But pretty uneventful?" Daniel asked. He held his breath waiting for the answer. It seemed there was something Alex wasn't telling him.

Marsha started the car from the passenger seat—either a sign that it was time to go; or the car was hot, and she needed the air.

"Yeah, really it was fine. But . . . "

*Oh no, here it comes.*

" . . . I just wanted to tell you, the other guy gave me this." He pulled money from his back pocket and handed it to Daniel.

*"A hundred dollars?* You're kidding!"

Alex's white teeth gleamed in the sunlight, and his dark eyes twinkled. "That's too much money to joke around about, Pastor."

Daniel held the bill, one side in each hand. He looked at it then back at Alex, over and over.

"The cost of the cameras," Alex said. "The Lord provides."

"He certainly does, my friend. He certainly does."

\* \* \*

For three days, there was no talk of Main Street Bar, except with his wife. Late at night, Daniel and Marsha laid in bed, discussing what might happen—whether or not he'd go to jail for punching Curtis or if the church might fire him. Neither seemed likely, but there were no guarantees. Then on Wednesday evening, an hour or so after the midweek service had ended, Daniel's cell phone rang, and that all-too-familiar number showed up on the screen.

"Hi, Pastor Whitefield. This is Joe. I got somebody here that could use a ride. You guys still up for it?"

Daniel paused for a moment. Were they still up for it? Homer had said they weren't done, and it was his night. He must've been right.

"Sure, Joe. I have a man on standby," Daniel said. "I'll let him know right away."

# Chapter Twenty-One

New Wine Transportation Company, Driver Log
Date: Wednesday, March 20
Driver: Homer Smith
Passenger: Gwen Smith

HOMER FIDDLED WITH THE CAMERA stuck to the dashboard. Pastor said it would stay put, but he wasn't so sure. And how would they see the picture if they needed to? Maybe the camera hooked up to a television somehow. The hi-tech gadget sure seemed out-of-place in his old car, with the wind-up windows and the cassette player. Then again, Homer was a little out-of-place himself. He hadn't been out of the house past nine o'clock since who-knows-when. But it felt right. Pastor had said a young lady needed a ride.

When he pulled in front of Main Street Bar and parked, he knew in an instant that he wouldn't need the hi-tech camera, anyway.

His passenger came slowly down the walkway, head down, shoulders hunched. She wore a white hoodie, and a hint of thick red bangs poked from underneath the hood. Even with the bulk of the sweatshirt, the girl was impossibly thin. Pale, white skin showed through the holes in her faded blue jeans. Halfway to the curb she looked up and froze.

Gwen pulled the hood off her head. The last time he saw her, she had long, wavy hair. Now it framed her face in a short, blunt bob. Her face was different, too, though a shadow of her former self remained.

The government called it an opioid crisis. Homer called it the devil. Nothing short of the devil himself could have changed his sweet Gwen in such a way—and not just in appearance. Six months, not even a phone call. No way to know if she was sick or had enough to eat. No way to know who she was with and how they treated her. No way to know if they'd see her again. Now, she was standing in front of him.

Homer's heart raced, and he held in a breath of relief so big, it pressed on his chest hard from the inside and almost came out in a shout.

"*Gwennie?*" he asked.

He hoisted a stiff leg onto the sidewalk and pulled the other up to join it. Then he started toward her, never looking away. He had to take in the sight of her every second he could. If she ran again, he'd miss it.

"I . . . I didn't really need a ride. That guy in there just offered," she said. She rocked from one foot to the other, then took a step backward. "He said someone could pick me up. I didn't know . . . I could have walked to a friend's house to crash. I . . . you . . . you don't have to take me."

"I've been praying for you, Gwen. Day and night." He reached the top of the two steps on the walkway. "Is it okay if I give you a hug?"

She said nothing but didn't step back. Homer closed the distance between them and wrapped his arms around Gwen, nestling his face against the side of hers. He choked down sobs of joy.

"Grandpa," she said, and the tears began to flow. She returned the hug but even tighter.

He was the first to pull away, but only in his hurry to get her out of the cold and into the warm car.

Homer offered Gwen his hand, but she shook her head no.

His heart sank in a sea of confusion.

*Please don't run. Lord, please don't let her run.*

He took a few slow sidesteps toward the car and stopped to watch her take a small one, then the same routine again and again. It was a strange dance. The war between heart and flesh, devotion and addiction played out in her feet.

Finally, they made it to the car, and she eased into the passenger seat next to him. As she closed the door, Homer's mind flashed to seven years earlier when she was sixteen. Every time she got into the car back then, she'd pull down the visor to check her lip gloss in the mirror. Every single time. So happy, full of life. And always wanting to look her best. Tonight, there was no lip gloss. There was no pocketbook or bag of any kind. And she didn't check the mirror.

Homer pulled away from the curb and started driving in no particular direction. He took a deep breath as he sent a silent prayer toward Heaven.

"Do you want to tell me where you've been?" he asked.

"No." She fidgeted beside him.

"Okay." He kept his voice soft and gentle. "Do you know where you want to go?"

"No." She turned toward the window.

"That's fine, Hummingbird. I've got a full tank of gas. We can drive all night if you want." And that was his plan. He'd drive until dawn and hit every street and country road in Springville if that's what it took for her to stay beside him just a little longer. Maybe he'd head north and hit the Blue Ridge Parkway, drive straight into Virginia. Just to be there with her.

It was several miles before either of them spoke again.

"Are you warm enough?" he asked.

"Yes."

"Good, good. I hope this is the last cold snap we'll have before spring. It's almost here."

He drove a couple more miles; then a faint sound caught his attention. The wind outside? No. It was Gwen sniffling, and the sound got louder as she turned toward him.

"Will you say it again, Grandpa?"

"Say what?"

"My nickname. What you use to call me when I was a little girl?"

His heart nearly burst out of his chest.

"Hummingbird. My little hummingbird."

He looked away from the road to see a tear run down her cheek.

"You used to flit from place to place so quick," he said, "hardly ever staying still. I love you, Hummingbird. Always have, always will."

She buried her face in her hands.

"I want to be that girl again, Grandpa," she cried. "I don't want to live like this anymore. I want to go home."

*Home.* The sweetest sound in the world. There'd be struggles to come, no doubt. Maybe even setbacks. But Homer's prayers had been answered.

"It's gonna be okay, Gwennie," he said. "We're gonna help you."

Homer brought the little white car to a stop in the middle of the deserted road and, looking over his shoulder, started a three-point turn. Now, he had a direction.

*Log Notes: I'm in awe of the goodness of my God tonight. He gave me the desire of my heart. I was called to give my prodigal grand-daughter a ride. Gwen came home with me, hopefully to stay, and what a time we had surprising her grandma.*

## Chapter Twenty-Two

WARM DAYS AND COLD NIGHTS. The month of March was fickle, like Daniel's life of late. Up and down. So many unknowns. Still, the Maker of the weather had His hand on all things, even legal matters, church business, and personal vendettas; and so much good had come along with the bad that Daniel could only be grateful for all of it.

On Friday morning, he sat in his usual booth with his favorite meal in front of him and familiar faces all around him, excited to share the good news with Speedy.

"Well, don't that beat all," Speedy said when Daniel relayed the story. "Praise the Lord."

"God is good," Daniel said with a smile, and he took another sip of coffee. "There's no way it was a coincidence that Homer got called out to pick up his granddaughter. No way in the world."

"Just more confirmation, idn't it? All this was meant to be?"

Daniel nodded, then took his last bite of biscuit and gravy and leaned back against the booth, satisfied.

"All of us have had calls now," Daniel said, "but I think Homer's may have been the most successful."

"Yes, sirree," Speedy said. "Seven calls in less than two weeks, when you didn't think you'd have many. That sure is somethin'."

*Seven calls. All seven of the men had gone out. The number seven.*

Daniel remembered Reggie Carson's words the day he'd came to visit. His stomach muscles tightened. That had to be it. That's what Reggie felt. The number seven was important because not only was it the number of men, it was also the number of jobs New Wine Transportation Company had to complete. Each of them with a unique purpose. Each of them a Divine appointment of some kind.

Daniel kept the revelation quiet, soaking in the peace of it. Whatever came, he could face it, knowing that their job was done and that they had done it well.

* * *

Daniel walked out of the diner and was greeted by warmth. The earthy smells of fresh grass and tilled soil met his nose and mingled with the restaurant odors that followed him out the door. He smiled at the sight of the staked garden at the little house across the street. Spring was here.

As he approached his parked Camry, his mood turned south. The left, front tire was completely flat.

*How in the world? A nail wouldn't have deflated it that fast.*

He hitched up his slacks at the knees and crouched beside the car to inspect the tire. His loafers creased across the toes as he positioned to get a better look. He ran his hand down the front over a four-inch gash. Intentionally cut. And there was only one person who could have done it.

Daniel stood and looked around. In broad daylight? Curtis was brazen. Maybe the gardener across the street had seen something.

The same rage Daniel had felt in the church study began to rise up. The tire wasn't such a big deal. Easily fixable. But why take it to this level? Why couldn't Curtis leave him alone? Anger turned to fear as Daniel thought of his wife. What if Curtis tried to hurt Marsha in some way? Claire was back at school, so at least she was away from the craziness. But Curtis had plenty of associates. What if he tried to get to her, too?

Daniel sat down in the driver seat and closed his eyes. With one foot outside on the ground and the other in the car, he leaned his head against the seat and prayed for his family's protection; then he drew a calming breath through his nose. Now to figure out what to do about the car.

It crossed Daniel's mind to call the sheriff's department, but after his recent run-in with the law, it seemed better to keep his distance.

The car hadn't come with a jack or a spare. Just a can of fix-a-flat. He'd have to call Roy at Springville Tire & Auto to come replace it, but that might take a while. How to get home now was the question; and since Marsha was at the hair salon and he didn't want to bother her, Daniel searched his brain for other options. Soon it came to him; he knew just whom to call.

*    *    *

"Harvey, I can't thank you enough," Daniel said as they turned into his driveway.

"Think nothing of it, Pastor," Harvey said.

How nice it had been to have a listening ear, to share about the note from Curtis and all that plagued Daniel's mind. Harvey had encouraged him to talk to law enforcement about the threat and the slashed tire—at least to Deputy Green—but he hadn't pushed.

"You've just been so supportive of me through everything," Daniel said.

Harvey smiled. "You've done a lot for my family over the years, not the least of which has been teaching us the Word of God. The way I see it, I'd be a pretty sorry sort of fella not to support my pastor, especially during the hard times."

Harvey put the SUV in Park, and Daniel reached to shake his hand, nearly double the size of his own.

"Well, just in case the deacon board does decide to fire me, I want you to know it's been a pleasure serving as your pastor." Daniel's heart ached at the sound of his own words.

Harvey let go of Daniel's hand and drew his head backward.

"*Fire you?* Nobody's said anything about firing you, Daniel. Why do you think that?"

"Well . . . I just . . . didn't the deacon board have an emergency meeting Saturday night? I assumed it was to vote on whether or not to fire me."

"We met, Daniel, but it was no emergency. Our normal meeting had to be rescheduled. That was the best time for everybody."

"Oh, that's right! The March meeting was canceled when Harold's back went out. I forgot!"

"I mean, we talked about you being arrested, of course. It's pretty big news. It's not every day the preacher gets arrested. But nobody said anything about firin'. We talked about who would fill in for the meantime if you have to go jail."

Daniel burst into laughter as relief washed over him.

"I figured you were still deciding. I've been worried all week." Daniel's stress poured out in continued laughter, until tears pooled in the corners of eyes. "I guess that will teach me to make assumptions."

"I guess so," Harvey said with a big smile, and he placed a hand on Daniel's shoulder.

Daniel thanked his friend again for the ride, and as he stepped from the car, he was hit by a strong, chilly wind that made him shiver. Up and down, like life. Yes, March was fickle.

# Chapter Twenty-Three

"I THINK YOU SHOULD APOLOGIZE," Marsha said.

Daniel sat up straight on the edge of the couch, causing Chewy to switch people. Marsha sat across from him in the arm chair, where she'd been reading.

"*Apologize?* To the person who caused me to be stranded at the diner? The person who left a threatening note at the church? The person who disrespected our daughter to my face and spread horrible rumors about you all over town?" He rubbed at the muscles in the back of his neck.

"Yes, and to the person you punched in the face," she said. "I just wonder if that's all it would take to end this. Maybe he'd drop this whole revenge thing."

"I don't think so, Marsha. Not someone like Curtis. He won't be satisfied so easily. And the punch isn't why he was mad in the first place."

"Maybe not, dear." She sighed and picked up her book again.

Daniel huffed and left the room, not sure where he was going. He stopped in the kitchen and poured a big glass of milk, then drank it too fast. A bubble of air caught in his throat and he swallowed hard to force it down; then he wiped his mouth with the back of his hand.

She was doing that thing—that thing where she suggested something, then pretended not to be sure that she was right, so he could mull over it and then still feel like it was his idea. But he was on to her. They'd been married too long for her reverse psychology to work on him.

He walked out onto the back deck and looked up at the stars, breathing in the crispness of the night. So many twinkling dots looked down on him. He stayed there for a while and let the tranquility of creation wrap him up and flood his spirit; then he went back inside the house. Down the hall and to the bedroom, Daniel made his way and found the slacks that he'd traded for sweat pants draped across the straight-back chair in the corner. He pulled his cell phone from the pocket and read the time on the display. 8:30 p.m.

The peaceful calm he'd felt outside had already slipped away, so he headed out again, gripping the phone as if he wanted to hurt it. Daniel paced the deck in his socked feet as he tapped the green phone icon and started dialing before he lost the nerve.

On the fourth ring, Curtis answered.

"What do *you* want?" he asked.

Daniel expected nothing more in way of a greeting. What exactly *had* he expected? He swallowed hard.

"Look, Curtis, I know that you are upset with me," Daniel said, "but I wanted—"

"You wanted to see if I'd give up my right to press charges, huh?"

"No, that's *not* what I was going to say." Daniel felt himself spiraling out of control but couldn't find the brakes. "But since we're talking about charges, what about finding my tire slashed today?"

"Oh, did you have some car trouble? I'm sorry to hear that." His tone was mocking.

"Don't act like you don't know. And I'm sure I could prove that it was you if I wanted to. Did you forget about the little note you left for me? Maybe you shouldn't have signed your name to it."

"*Ha*. That wouldn't prove anything, except that I wanted to get under your skin. Apparently, it worked. Now listen, I'm heading back to Charlotte tomorrow, but you can guarantee you'll be hearing from my lawyer. Goodbye, *Preacher*."

The call disconnected, and Daniel slammed his fist against the deck railing. Pain pulsed through it, just under the surface. When the anger had reduced from boiling to simmer, he went back inside. He'd have to battle the urge like a prize-fighter—the urge to tell his wife that she was wrong.

* * *

Throughout the night, Daniel's dreams disturbed him. An alarm clock sounded in the first dream, causing him to wake up and get out of bed. He thought it was morning until the darkness outside told him otherwise and he checked the time on his phone. 1:00 a.m. More of the same followed, and he had to will himself back to sleep over and over, each time taking longer.

When the light outside his window was pink and orange instead of black, he gave up and got out of bed. He prayed until the sun didn't touch the horizon; and by the time Marsha woke up, Daniel was dressed and ready to go.

She ran her fingers through a fluffy mass of dark curls on top of her head and stretched.

"What are you doing up so early?" she asked.

Daniel crossed the room and sat on the edge of the bed next to her.

"He's headed back to Charlotte today. I have to go apologize."

Marsha sat up straight.

"Are you sure?" she asked.

"Weren't you the one who suggested it?"

"Well, yes, but I just want to make sure you're doing it because you really *want* to and not because of me."

"Marsha," he said, taking her hand, "I love you with all my heart; but trust me—I wouldn't be doing this just because you said so. I think I'd rather get a root canal than to face Curtis. But you were right. Not about it fixing anything. I don't think that will happen. But I still need to do it. Whether he hears me or not." He looked toward the ceiling. "Heaven help me."

She reached to hold him, then whispered to him gently, "'[You] can do all things through Christ who strengthens [you].'"[15] She pulled away and grinned. "A little cliché?"

"Yes." Daniel stood, wagging his head and smiling. "But it's still true. You know it is."

"Want me to go with you?"

"And give him the opportunity to eyeball you again? Not a chance." He kissed her on the head. "I'll be fine, sweetie. Be back before you know it."

---

15   Philippians 4:13

# Chapter Twenty-Four

A FEW WEEKS IN A *hotel. That's pricey,* Daniel thought as he pulled into the parking lot of the Springville Inn. *At least one of Curtis's businesses must be doing well.* He tried to swallow the bit of jealousy that rose up in him.

A gentle mist began to fall, and fine droplets dotted the windshield. Daniel put the Camry into Park. The clock in the dash read 8:02 a.m. *I hope I didn't miss him. And I hope he's not asleep,* he thought.

Daniel whispered a quick, final prayer and reached for the door handle. When the door was open only an inch, a patrol car whipped into the space beside him. Daniel tensed. Was he there for him? No, that was silly. He looked around. Another car pulled into the space on the other side of him. A sheriff's deputy emerged from each car, and they converged at the front of Daniel's vehicle. Neither looked at him.

In the rearview mirror, he saw two more patrol cars parked on the other side of the lot. A knot formed in Daniel's stomach. What could be going on?

He sat there as the officers went through the front door of the hotel together; then he breathed a sigh of relief. Strange how one arrest could make a preacher so jittery, but nerves didn't observe logic. Now his concern was how *not* to get in the middle of any legal matters that might be going on inside. He'd simply have to wait them out.

Five minutes, ten minutes, fifteen minutes passed, and he grew more and more anxious to get the job over with and get back home. Marsha would be worried. And if Curtis wouldn't talk to him on the phone, he had to clear his conscience face-to-face. After twenty minutes in the car, he couldn't wait any longer.

Daniel marched to the front door, head down in concentration, rehearsing how it should go down. *Curtis, I'm sorry I punched you. I shouldn't have lost my temper. I hope you'll forgive me.* If it felt right and if he had any gumption left, he'd talk to him about God.

He reached for the door. Not automatic like in newer places. One foot in the lobby, he saw them. The officers from the parking lot came toward him in a huddle, accompanied by other uniformed men. In the middle of the crowd of officers was Curtis, his hands behind his back.

Daniel's brain went numb, and he stood there like a doorman as they exited. Curtis didn't look up to notice him. No one acknowledged Daniel at all until the last man in the group passed by.

"Pastor Whitefield."

Daniel focused on the man's face and tried to place it.

"I'm surprised to see you here," the officer said. He wore a dark suit, like a businessman, but he wore a shiny badge on his lapel.

The voice. Daniel knew the voice well.

"Joe?"

"Agent Joseph Spence. FBI." Joe stuck out his hand.

Shock flooded Daniel's mind. It couldn't be.

"But...?"

"Come with me, Pastor. I'll explain."

Daniel stayed close on his heels as they walked to an unmarked car. A deputy helped Curtis into the backseat as the others headed for their own patrol cars. "Suspect apprehended without incident." The deputy spoke into a radio attached to his shirt as he shut the door.

Joe signaled to the deputy, then turned to Daniel and leaned against the car.

"*FBI?*" Daniel said.

"I know this will be a lot to take in, and there's much I can't disclose. But we've had an eye on Mr. Curtis for quite some time. I've been working undercover trying to establish a case against him."

"A case for what?"

"Like I said, some if it's classified. But the main focus was illegal gambling."

"*What?* He had a gambling operation at the bar?"

Joe grinned and nodded.

"And what about the other investigation?" Daniel said "The underage drinking."

"Well, let's just say, we would have already shut him down if that's all we were after. But we couldn't risk the operation. You see, Curtis is a little guy in a very big pond, and we need him to help us nab some bigger fish. He manages businesses for some pretty shady characters."

"*Manages?* You mean he doesn't own them?"

"Not that we've been able to find. He's a lackey."

"It's so hard to believe. All the times you called me, as the manager of the bar . . . "

Joe chuckled.

"We have another agent working undercover, too. One of your men gave him a ride here the other night."

"Alex."

"Yep. And we borrowed the video from his dash cam to add to our pile of evidence. He turned it in to the sheriff's department. They've been helping us."

"So, the hundred dollar tip came from him."

Joe only smiled.

"Okay, Reverend Whitefield, I gotta hit the road."

He ducked and looked to check on his associate in the car. Daniel stole a glance at Curtis in the backseat. His face was still pointed toward the floor.

"I know you need to get going, Agent Spence, but there's so much more I'd like to know. Wednesday night. That girl didn't ask for a ride, did she? You were trying to help her. And the first time you called me, I bet you were just looking out for that kid, too."

Daniel's mind raced with questions. Never in a million years could he have imagined things playing out like this.

Joe shrugged. "Eh, just seemed like a good idea."

Modest answer, but Joe wasn't fooling him.

The agent opened the car door and sat down with one leg still outside.

"Funny thing is," Joe said, "he got so much attention from those church folks, he almost shut it down before it got started. And we wouldn't have a case. But they can be happy now. Main Street Bar is out of business."

Curtis looked up, seeming to notice Daniel for the first time.

Daniel fixed his eyes on Curtis's face. Defeated. Tired. For a moment, he saw his old college roommate—an intelligent, business-minded, young man. Somewhere, his ambitions had taken a turn.

"I'm sorry, Reverend. We really need to be going," Joe said.

"Um . . . can I talk to him? Just for a second."

Joe looked over his shoulder, then back at Daniel.

"Make it quick."

Daniel shoved his hands into his jacket pockets and stepped back from the car for a better view.

"Curtis . . . I just want to tell you, I'm sorry. I'm sorry for what happened last week. I shouldn't have punched you." The words tasted worse than Daniel expected.

Curtis tilted his head and raised an eyebrow, then slowly turned toward the window. Daniel waited, but Curtis didn't look at him again.

*Say something*, Daniel thought. *Anything.*

There was nothing more he could say or do. It was like being next in line after waiting for hours, then finding out the ride is closed for maintenance.

"Oh, by the way, that was quite a right hook you threw, Reverend." Joe's face held the biggest grin yet. "But I think we can help with your court case. Don't give it another thought."

Daniel closed his eyes tightly and drew a deep breath. *Could it really be over?*

He nodded his thanks at Joe and took one last look at the detainee. His heart ached. Maybe one day, Curtis would find his way. Maybe one day, Curtis would find God's way.

Joe closed the car door. After a moment, he backed away from the curb and pointed the car toward the highway. The rain picked up again as Joe stopped and rolled down his window.

"One last thing that might interest you."

Daniel stepped closer. How could there possibly be more?

"We heard something about a note Curtis left for you. On Sunday? A deputy who's been helping with the case made us aware. Your arresting officer, actually."

*Jason.*

"Communicating threats is a crime, too," Joe said. "You can expect to see that on the list of charges when it's made public."

*Harvey must have told Jason about the note.*

Daniel didn't mention the tire, in case Joe didn't already know. He put a hand over his face and slid it slowly downward, tracing the contour of his jaw. Stubble pricked his fingers. Then his arm went heavy, and he dropped it to his side.

"Thank you again, Agent Spence. I'm just so . . . I don't even know—"

"You can call me Joe." The agent smiled. "It's a nice, little town you got here, Preacher. I wish you the best."

Daniel stood there, mist accumulating on his jacket but floodwaters rushing over his soul as the car drove away. The silhouette of Curtis's head through the back glass became smaller and smaller, and Daniel prayed for him until they were out of sight.

The honk of a horn startled Daniel out of his daze. He was standing in the middle of the parking lot in the direct path of a Lincoln Town Car. He waved an apology to the driver and stumbled toward his own vehicle. Daniel rubbed at his temples, scratching himself with the car key he hadn't realized was in his hand.

Back at the car, the clock on the dash read 8:36. His phone lay in the seat beside him. Two missed calls from Marsha. No doubt, she was worried, though it hadn't been long. He could just imagine her reaction when he called on the way home and told her everything that had happened. And the men. He had to tell each of them, as soon as possible. Maybe he'd schedule another meeting to break the news. All along, they'd thought New Wine Transportation Company was a ministry of seven. But they were wrong. There were actually *eight*, and each had been called for a very specific purpose, part of which might never be known this side of eternity: Daniel, Homer, Harvey, Stewart, Nikolas, Alex, Greg, and Joe.

The brain fog continued to lift as he backed out of the parking space. So many calls or visits to make. Reggie and Speedy would want to know, too.

*It's not gossip if it's true, right?*

He shook his head, the shock of what had happened still fresh. When he came to a stop sign and with no cars behind him, he sent Marsha a text.

*All is well. On my way home. Will tell you all about it then. Love you much.*

He looked both ways, preparing to turn left to head to the highway, but as a last-second decision, he steered to the right instead. Main Street was calling him, and a quick detour through downtown wouldn't hurt. It was the destination that mattered most.

*Epilogue*

DANIEL'S FAVORITE DAY ON THE calendar had arrived—Easter Sunday. The air was alive with hope because the resurrection made the impossible *possible*. It reversed the curse that all men were destined to suffer, and the church rejoiced collectively for the pardon.

Easter Sunday brought a crowd almost matching Christmas. New faces and long-time-no-see faces floated through the congregation with the regulars, all wearing smiles reflecting their shared joy. Even the doubters wore the glow, infected by the glorious truth—He's alive.

Since the crowd was so large and the day so beautiful, Daniel and Marsha took their meeting and greeting outside at the close of the service to just beyond the church doors.

Little girls in frilly socks and big flowered hats and little boys in bow ties and shiny shoes rushed past them, baskets in tow, headed to the churchyard to hunt for Easter eggs. Claire had taken on the responsibility of hiding the eggs, and she stood at the far side of the yard waiting for the children, pretty as a painting. It seemed like only yesterday, she was carrying a basket herself, and Daniel loved each Easter memory of her.

Watching the festive scene, Daniel thought of Homer and Rachel. How he missed them. They both loved Easter Sunday service, just as he did, but it was visiting day at the rehab center, and

Gwen had requested a rhubarb pie. It was also the perfect time for them to deliver care packages for all the patients, courtesy of the newly-formed Men's Ministry League—a group which included all seven participants of New Wine Transportation Company, plus a dozen more men.

After the children, the next to exit the church was the Martinez family.

"Happy Easter," Daniel said to Alex and his parents. "Say, Alex, were you able to make that delivery we discussed? What did they say?"

Mr. and Mrs. Martinez smiled proudly.

"Oh, yes, Pastor," Alex said. "Mrs. Johnson at the children's home was happy to get the cameras. She said they could definitely find a good use for them."

"Wonderful! Thank you for dropping them off."

They shook hands a second time, and Alex walked away.

More congregants filed out and found their places in the sea of neck-hugging, back-slapping, and hand-shaking. *Visiting.* Sunday after service was a time for visiting. And a holiday made it all the more special.

Daniel and Marsha greeted the choir director and the piano player, the Sunday school teachers, the deacons, laypeople of all sorts, and friends old and new.

Agnes Reynolds came by, stopping briefly to tell Daniel that the sermon had been a bit long. He looked at her thoughtfully for a moment, then scooped her up in a big hug. "Thank you for that feedback, Agnes," Daniel said. "I don't know what I'd do without you." Wiggling from his embrace, she hurried away, and Marsha stifled a giggle.

Next in line were the lovebirds. Three Sunday mornings in a row, they'd left church arm-in-arm, and Daniel could almost hear the wedding bells in the air already.

"Monica, I love your hat," Marsha said.

The brim of the navy headwear brushed against Stewart's hair as they walked, but if it bothered him, he didn't show it.

"Thank you, Mrs. Whitefield," Monica said.

"Now, I told you to call me Marsha. We're all good friends."

Monica thanked her, and Stewart's face added blushing cheeks to its huge smile as he led her to the car.

The crowd thinned, and Marsha leaned over and kissed Daniel's cheek when no one was looking. "I'm going to go call Richard and Diane. Let them know we'll be over for lunch soon."

"Okay, sweetie."

He admired his bride as she walked away in her flowy, cream-colored dress. Then someone to his left redirected his attention.

"Pastor Whitefield," the man said.

His face was unfamiliar, but Daniel knew the woman and the two children who grouped around the man as if he was a celebrity.

"Good morning and Happy Easter," Daniel said. "Good to have you with us."

T.J. returned the greeting and introduced himself. "I . . . uh . . . I'd like to talk to you sometime, Preacher. In private, if that's okay. Do you think we could set something up soon?"

Daniel reached for his wallet, pulled out a card, and handed it to T.J.

"I'm happy to meet with you. Call anytime."

T.J. nodded his thanks and headed to the parking lot, wrapping his arms around his daughters' shoulders as he went.

Jennifer stayed behind, and placing a hand on Daniel's arm, she whispered with excitement, "He wants to know if the church can help get an AA group started. Maybe meet here." She beamed at him, her eyes glimmering with tears; then she hurried to catch up with her family.

Daniel watched them as they got into their car. Miracle of miracles. God was still changing lives. And he rejoiced inside for each of them, especially the children.

"Thank you, Lord," he whispered.

Daniel took a few steps back and studied the front of the church, with its wooden double doors opened wide. Springville Community Christian Church was much more than a place of worship. Much more than a building. It was his life's calling. The place God had planted him to serve. And he'd keep on serving there, for as long as God allowed. In the mundane and in the magnificent, he'd stay the course. If the tasks were easy or Isaac-on-the-altar hard, he'd obey.

*What other way is there?*

*Love does no harm to a neighbor; therefore love is the fulfillment of the law.*

*And do this, knowing the time, that now it is high time to awake out of sleep; for now our salvation is nearer than when we first believed.*

*The night is far spent, the day is at hand. Therefore let us cast off the works of darkness, and let us put on the armor of light.*

*Let us walk properly, as in the day, not in revelry and drunkenness, not in lewdness and lust, not in strife and envy.*

*But put on the Lord Jesus Christ, and make no provision for the flesh, to fulfill its lusts.*

Romans 13:10-14

# Author's Note

In my first book, *Grace & Lavender*, I used each of my children's names in some way, just for fun; but I had no idea that a minor character in that book would later become the main character in another book. That's why the preacher in this story and my son have the same name—Daniel. As it turns out, it was a perfect name for the character of Daniel Whitefield, who focuses on what the Lord, and not man, thinks of him, because the name means "God is my judge."

This story is a bit unique, and perhaps a bit of a risk, in the fact that there are no female point-of-view characters. Also, because there is only one point of view character for the majority of the book, yet six minor characters take over the story for a chapter each. I hope readers will appreciate this deviation from convention.

Whether or not all of the main characters' views align with your own, I hope you see the love of God in the lives of Daniel and Marsha Whitefield. Most importantly, I hope you are able to recognize and accept His love in your own life. There is no greater decision you can make than choosing to believe in and follow Jesus.

Thank you for reading. I look forward to, hopefully, creating more stories about the people of Springville, North Carolina.

A SPRINGVILLE STORY
Grace
&
Lavender
a novel
Heather Norman Smith

Recently retired Colleen Hill is always busy, constantly on a quest to make life more interesting.

When the ladies' group at her church partners with the local children's home, Colleen jumps in as usual, volunteering to share her passion for cooking with a troubled teenager named Grace. But Colleen must balance the new project with her pursuit of becoming a contestant on a television game show, along with all the other ideas her brain continually spins out.

Colleen's daughter Melody is quite different. She lives a calm, simple life and is content with who she is. That is, until an unexpected opportunity to work with Grace, too, pushes her to reevaluate life and dare to take on bigger dreams. The path starts with a newly-found interest in soap-making and leads her to responsibilities she didn't even know she wanted, including helping Grace understand the meaning of her name.

*Grace & Lavender* is a book for all audiences—a heart-warming story that reminds us to seek God's purpose for our lives.

# WHERE I WAS PLANTED

Heather Norman Smith

In the spring of 1961, ten-year-old Nate "Weenie" Dooley has a revelation-his father is not a good one.

Inspired by *National Geographic*, his favorite thing next to the Bible storybook his mother gave him before she died, Nate plans to leave his father and their home in the Smokies to set out on adventure. When he discovers that his father has left him first, it will take the help of a stray dog, some kind neighbors, a one-man-band, letters from a long-lost-aunt, and a new understanding of God to figure out he isn't really alone.

Will he find that Copper Creek is where he's always belonged? Or will his wanderlust keep him from ever coming back?

In her second novel, Heather Norman Smith demonstrates that love makes a family, and that while fathers may leave, our Heavenly Father is faithful, and He has a plan for all of us.

For more information about
**Heather Norman Smith**
&
*New Wine Transportation Company*
please visit:

www.heathernormansmith.com
@HNSblog
www.facebook.com/heathernormansmith
www.instagram.com/heathernormansmith

For more information about
AMBASSADOR INTERNATIONAL
please visit:

*www.ambassador-international.com*
*@AmbassadorIntl*
*www.facebook.com/AmbassadorIntl*

*Thank you for reading this book. Please consider leaving us a review on your favorite retailer's website, Goodreads or Bookbub, or our website.*

Made in the USA
Columbia, SC
29 April 2021

36497524R00108